Salamander

Salamander

Roger Silverwood

ROBERT HALE · LONDON

Robert Hale Limited
Clerkenwell House
Clerkenwell Green
London EC1R 0HT

Typeset in 11.25/15pt Janson
Printed in Great Britain by St Edmundsbury Press
Bury St Edmunds, Suffolk
Bound by Woolnough Bookbinding Limited

ONE

Ward 12, Castlecombe General Hospital, North Yorkshire, UK, 12 August 2001.

An energetic nurse rammed the treatment trolley through the door of the private ward and up to the side of the bed. 'Come along, Frank,' she bawled. 'Waken up. Waken up. It's all over now. You're back from theatre.'

The man in the bed didn't move; he was in the Land of Nod and in no hurry to leave it.

The nurse grabbed his wrist and peered down at a watch suspended from her pocket. After a few seconds, she dropped the wrist and pulled the trolley nearer to the bed.

'Come along. Wakey wakey. I've twenty-eight really *sick* people needing my attention. Just because your face is all over the television doesn't mean you are entitled to any special treatment!'

The man sighed, lifted one eyelid minimally and peered through the anaesthetic at the disinfected blue-and-white-clad, noisy whirlwind, jigging around the treatment trolley, annoyingly disturbing the quiet and causing the bed to shake.

A stinging pain in his stomach reminded him of why he

SALAMANDER

was there. He bent his knees slightly and shuffled his ankles and feet under the tight blankets, trying to find a comfortable position.

'Come along, Frank,' she said more urgently.

He scowled at her and muttered something that sounded like 'sugar off' but was not as sweet.

Brandishing a stethoscope, she snapped the rubber gloves at the wrists, advanced to the head of the bed and looked into his face.

'Let's have your arm,' she ordered.

He didn't move. He licked his lips.

'I'd like a drink. A bottle of Old Peculier ...'

'Don't be silly, Frank,' she said and began to roll up his sleeve.

He wrinkled his nose and peered at her through one eye. 'Who *are* you?' he muttered.

'Don't tell me you don't recognize *me*?'

She wrapped the sphygmomanometer cuff round the top of his arm.

'No,' he grunted and ran his parched tongue round what felt like a bag of feathers.

His head dropped on to his chest. His eyes closed.

The cuff round his arm was getting tighter and more annoying as she repeatedly squeezed the bulb.

He pulled a face.

'I'm Maisie,' she said assertively.

'Maisie?' he muttered weakly and shook his head. His eyes stayed closed.

'Stop pulling away,' she said. 'Put your arm straight out in front of you.'

She put the stethoscope to her ears.

'I've got an itch,' he said, pulling it away and reaching up to the top of his head.

'Wait until I've finished.'

He struggled with her momentarily but he wasn't strong enough. He surrendered, groaned and flopped back against the pillows.

She looked at him and smiled, and listened to the pulse on his arm.

'Maisie? Did you say Maisie?' he asked foggily.

She released the air in the cuff, put the stethoscope on the trolley and wrote the numbers on a clipboard. She looked into his half-closed eyes and shook her head. 'Maisie Dowdeswell. I'm married now ... Well, I *was* ... Got two boys and a girl. *Used* to be Henderson. My father's the dentist. I won't believe you if you say you've forgotten *me*!'

His jaw dropped. His eyes opened and he peered at her. 'Maisie Henderson? Never!' He blinked. 'Why, we used to sit on the back seat in the Empire,' he began, then smiled. 'You used to let me squeeze your—'

Her eyes flashed.

'That's a long time ago, Frank,' she burst in quickly. She looked round at the door behind her.

'Maisie Henderson ... Three kids, eh?'

'Don't say *any more*, Frank Norman Spence. Don't say *any more*!'

'It's a wonder you haven't got your own football team,' he said, trying to smile through the pain. He looked up at her and cast his mind back two decades. 'Maisie Henderson,' he said incredulously and shook his head. 'You've changed. You *have* changed. You *used* to be a good looker.'

'Oh!' she gasped angrily. 'You've changed *too*,' she retaliated. 'And not for the better. *My*, you've put on some weight.' She pointed to his navel. 'That's not a six-pack – more like a cask.' She tugged roughly at the cuff round his arm and whisked the sphygmomanometer away.

His head had dropped on his chest. His eyes closed.

'I'm going to give you something for the pain,' she said. 'And to shut you up.'

She turned to the trolley and picked up a hypodermic.

He suddenly opened his eyes and in a loud, clear voice said, 'Where's my wife?'

Maisie shook her head.

'She's all right. They've taken her to the police station. This hospital isn't safe for *her* to be here. It's not safe for *anybody* to be here. The whole building is overrun with *you* lot. There are police with guns all over the place. There's two outside this door and there's a whole bunch on the roof. They've turned the laundry room into *Mission Control*. It's all on account of you. I don't know what the blazes you've done, or how you collected that bullet! This isn't a hospital any more, it's more like a war zone!'

She plunged the needle into his arm.

'Ahhhhh,' he groaned softly and went straight back to Nod.

The Glass Palace, 4m NNW of Baghdad, 31 March 2003, 1.59 a.m

There was no moon and no stars: the sky was blacker than a joiner's thumbnail. In the hot, dusty and miserable darkness, Baghdad's bomb-damaged minarets, hotels, government offices, houses and streets were still and quiet. The only sound was the persistent howling of two dogs.

Four men in desert issue British Army uniforms scrambled silently among the dusty debris in the courtyard of the famous Glass Palace. Rivulets of sweat ran down their faces. Three of them wore big packs and carried SA80s, their sweaty fingers hovering nervously over the triggers. The

fourth, an officer, carried a black rubber torch, and a Beretta
92. They advanced in short spurts towards the marble steps
of the massive overbearing palace entrance. There was
nobody around. No guards. No opposition. No Iraqis. No
Americans. The only adversary was the environment:
Baghdad was the kitchen of hell with the oven door wide
open.

The officer flashed the torch to the back of his wrist. He
whispered, 'Thirty seconds. Let's get inside.'

The men scrambled silently to the top of the steps and
looked up at the huge double doors of the Glass Palace. The
officer flashed up the torch. Gold embossed dragons and
other symbolic emblems glowed back at them. Rough pieces
of marble and stone masonry littered the doorway from
earlier bombing. They scrambled over the debris and
together pushed hard against the doors. They didn't budge.
They tried again. They didn't even shake.

'See to it, Shorty,' the officer whispered impatiently.

The smallest man of the four rolled the big pack off his
back and unfastened the straps. He fumbled inside it and
pulled out a 2 kg pack of plastic explosive and a small
wooden container the size of a cigar box. He peeled the
greaseproof paper from the Semtex, selected a detonator
from the box, jabbed it into the plastic and began to mould
the clammy stuff round the door and door jamb where he
thought a hinge would be.

In the distance a clock struck two.

The men looked towards each other and then expectantly
at the sky.

The deep drone of airplanes could be heard faintly
approaching from the south. A distant siren began to wail,
then another, nearer, then a third nearer still.

A minute later all hell was let loose.

The whistle of bombs and land-mines followed by mighty explosions, mostly over the city centre four miles away, battered the hot night; several fell a few hundred yards away, causing the palace steps to shake.

'Ready,' Shorty called to the three men crouched on the steps.

The officer turned away from looking at the sky. 'Take cover.'

The men crouched at the bottom of the steps, behind the balustrade. Shorty joined them. He took a remote sensor out of his top pocket, pointed it at the detonator, pressed the button and lowered his head.

There was one short, sharp, hell of a bang.

The marble step beneath them vibrated, their ears closed off for a second or two. Plaster and dust showered down, rattling their helmets.

Behind them, in the palace yard, a small fire had broken out, the result of an incendiary landing on the royal stables. Yellow flames from it illuminated the gold-painted railings and white plaster walls.

The men looked up, and as the dust cleared they could see that the door was sufficiently dislodged and set askew to permit their access. They rushed up the steps and through the gap into a corridor inside the mammoth building. The mighty bang of a bomb close by caused the shaking of the floor, and the fall of plaster accompanied them as they ran down the long corridor and through huge open doors at the end. The officer flashed the torch round and up the walls of the richly decorated cathedral-like building. The big windows on three sides no longer boasted coloured glass designs. The glass had been blown out. One large chair at the top of six steps dominated the far end. Lumps of brick, stone and plasterwork were strewn everywhere on the marble floor and steps. Looters had apparently already taken everything that wasn't screwed down or cemented to the floors or walls. A few short lengths of carpet had been ripped up and, as a result of gratuitous thievery, lay abandoned in small piles here and there.

The officer pointed to the big throne and the men raced across the hall and up the steps to it.

Behind the throne, long velvet curtains hung raggedly, half covering two large black wooden panels. He shone the torch up to the top of the curtains. He tugged at them and pulled them to one side, creating a shower of dust. He spat out the dust and irritably banged his Beretta on a panel.

'It's behind there.'

The men advanced on it aggressively, knocking and kicking it to see how it might be shifted. It didn't budge. They looked from one to the other. There was no easy way.

'Quickest would be to blow it.'

The officer nodded.

'Not too much, Shorty. Just enough to ... dislodge them.'

The man began to unload his big pack again.

The officer tapped on the wooden panels and ran his torch up and down. He came away shaking his head.

The other two squatted by the huge throne, fingering the trigger guards of their SA80s while gazing into the darkness of the huge palatial room. They looked beyond through the big, glassless windows, at the display of red and yellow explosions in the night sky, accompanied by the sounds of falling bombs, explosions and the collapse of buildings. The scale and intensity of the barrage was difficult to under-stand; they stood there, avoiding each other's eyes, in unbelieving, sober silence, and wished they were anywhere else but there.

'Take cover!' the officer yelled.

They scrambled down the steps and pressed against the wall.

There was another bang. The black wooden doors were blown away in small bits, and a moment later, half a ton of chiselled marble crashed down on to the throne: plaster and stone flew off in all directions. The fall came where seconds earlier they had been standing. It had come down from the ceiling directly above.

'Hell fire!' one of the men yelled.

They all sighed quietly but said nothing. They would be glad to get out of this death trap.

It took half a minute for the yellow dust to clear and then the officer flashed the torch where the black doors had been. They advanced up the steps and saw a huge metal wheel, a metre in diameter, set vertically into a large, black, steel door, which had two brass handles, two large keyholes with polished brass surrounds and a brass nameplate. The officer held the torch on it while they stared at it thoughtfully. Shorty took the torch and looked closely at the nameplate.

'It's English,' he said. 'London 1966. British. It's a Staveley. Hmm.'

'Can you get into it, that's the thing?'

'Maybe. I don't know,' he said, rubbing his greasy chin. 'That casing could be a foot thick.' He put his hands on the wheel and attempted to turn it in an anti-clockwise direction. He tried a clockwise direction. It didn't budge either way.

'Best thing I can do is try and blow the lock ... both locks.'

He dived into the big pack. He pulled out some Semtex, tore off a piece and began rolling it between his hands into the shape of spaghetti.

'I've got to be careful not to damage the screw mechanism. If I do, even if I manage to blow the locks open, we won't be able to open it.'

'Is that the best bet?'

'It's the *only* bet.'

'Right,' the officer said.

Shorty fed a length of the worm shape into each keyhole. He then built up a small wodge of Semtex over the keyholes and stuck a detonator into each.

Two minutes later, it was all done.

'It's ready, sir. Cross your fingers.'

'Take cover.'

They moved down the steps and round the corner by the wall again. They leaned back against it, gripping their SA80s with both hands.

Shorty took out the remote sensor, pointed it at the detonators and pressed the button.

There were two much smaller simultaneous explosions. A second later, there was the almighty sound of more debris falling. They felt the powerful blast of air and the wave of dust shower over them. Nobody could see what had happened. They squinted anxiously at each other as the air cleared.

Shorty looked doubtful, licked his lips and spat out the dust.

'Stay here,' the officer said. 'Wait until it settles.' He switched on the torch. The throne was covered in debris. He shone the light upwards. Another chunk of decorated marble vaulting had fallen. There was a big grey patch and new cracks had appeared in the white arched ceiling. He turned the torch on to the vault; dust was still swirling round the door. The wheel was becoming visible again.

'Do you want to do the honours, Shorty?'

The little man went gingerly up the steps, rubbed his hands together, reached out for the wheel and attempted to turn it. He tried each direction. It didn't respond. It was very stiff. He gave it a strong pull anti-clockwise and it suddenly began to move. He pulled again and it moved again. His face brightened.

'It's moving, sir,' he yelled excitedly. 'It's only bloody moving!' he cried, excitement bursting out of him.

At that moment, there was a loud explosion of a heavy bomb close by. It was from the palace yard. The floor shook. Everything shook. More dust fell.

The officer sucked in air and shone the torch up at the ceiling.

'Take cover, Shorty!'

Another massive lump of marble began to fall. He saw it getting bigger as if he was seeing trick camera work on a disaster movie.

'Take cover!' he yelled again, frantically, and dashed back to the wall.

Shorty gasped. His arms turned to goose-flesh, his spine to jelly. He leaned forward and hugged the wheel.

The other three men pressed hard back against the wall then froze, and prayed.

A huge chunk of the ceiling dropped behind the throne and down the middle of the big room. The entire building shook as it landed. A cloud of dust twenty feet high swirled, rose up, hung in the room like a cloud, and then slowly, mysteriously fell to the floor.

It went quiet: silent as the grave.

The officer brushed dust off his mouth and eyes and dashed up the steps to the vault; the other two followed. The young one was coughing up plaster dust as he stumbled up the steps.

The officer reached the engineer first.

'Are you all right, Shorty?'

The engineer was hanging on to the wheel, his head

drooping and his knees bent. There was debris on the floor close by him. He didn't reply. His eyes were closed.

The youngest man grabbed him by his arm. 'He isn't breathing!' he said.

The officer said, 'Put him down here.'

They disentangled him from the wheel and gently lowered him to the floor.

'Shorty!' he called desperately and patted his face.

The big man put down his SA80 and dragged over his big pack as a makeshift pillow.

The officer put his hand to his neck. He couldn't find a pulse.

'Is he going to be all right?'

'Shorty!'

The officer tried for a pulse again.

The youngest shone a torch into his face and gently brushed away the dust from his lips.

'Give him a drink.'

'It's too late. I think he's gone.'

Shorty groaned and shook his head.

They sighed with relief.

He raised a hand to his mouth and began to spit out bits of plaster and dust. He shook his head.

'Are you all right, Shorty? Are you hurt?'

'I don't know,' he groaned.

One of them reached for his water bottle and held it to his lips. The engineer was glad to have a drink.

'Ta.'

'Let's move away from here,' the officer said, glancing up at the ceiling.

Shorty began to wriggle his arms, his shoulders, his legs and then his fingers. Then he pulled a face of pain.

'Can you walk?'

'Yeah. I think so,' he said, shaking his head. 'Something heavy belted me in the back.'

They helped him to his feet. He stood there, feet set wide apart, swaying, holding his back. They held on to him.

'I'm OK. I'm OK,' he said, suddenly pulling away from them ungraciously.

'Go round the corner and rest up,' the officer said. 'If there's another bomb, all the bloody roof might come down.'

Shorty suddenly remembered what he had been about before the big fall. He ignored the order.

'The vault's unlocked!' he cried. He turned round and staggered up to the big wheel and began turning it.

The three men closed in on him and watched. The big man gave him a hand to speed up the action. They had all forgotten the fall and the danger; their eyes glowed in anticipation.

The two men turned the wheel through six revolutions then there was a quiet clunk. It wouldn't turn any more. Shorty looked up at the other three.

'That's it,' he whispered, hardly believing it. '*It's unlocked.*'

The young man and the big man leaned forward, grabbed the brass handles of the huge vault door and pulled. The hinges squealed as it opened.

The officer shone the torch inside. There was a bank of sixty small drawers in a green enamelled metal chest. On top of the drawers was a solitary brown leather jewel case about 20" x 10" x 8". His eyes lit up as he spotted it. His pulse raced. He leaned in and grabbed it.

'This'll be it.'

The others closed in. He gave the torch to Shorty while he unfastened the loops. His hands were shaking and his fingers were all thumbs as he excitedly lifted the jewel case lid.

Shorty shone the torch into the case.

They all gasped as they saw a glittering, almost blinding, show of diamonds and rubies set in lapis lazuli sculpted to represent a reptile.

The diamonds twinkled as the torch in Shorty's hand shook with uncontrolled excitement.

None of them had ever seen anything as stunning.

'The Salamander!' the officer said breathily and his eyes glazed over, as in his imagination he was transported back a hundred years to the Persia of vast riches, omnipotent power and stunningly beautiful women with faces tantalizingly hidden behind yashmaks.

'Wow.'

The four men stood in silence, mesmerized by the splendour and wonder of the jewel.

At length, the youngest one said, 'What do you reckon we can get for it?'

There was an explosion in the distance.

It broke the spell.

The officer dropped the lid.

'Let's get out of here,' he whispered as he began to fasten the straps.

The big man said, 'What's in the drawers?'

The young man pulled one open. It was very tightly packed with something. He dug in his fingers and pulled out a fistful of paper. It was Iraqi currency with the figure 100 and pictures of Saddam Hussein prominently represented on a cream-coloured background. He opened another drawer: it contained more of the same.

The officer shook his head. 'Nobody will want that stuff now.'

There was another explosion in the distance.

Some dust fell down on them.

The young man urgently tried to shove the money back in the drawer. It wouldn't fit.

'Come on,' the officer said, shoving the leather case firmly under his arm. 'Let's get out of here.'

The young man stuffed the wodge of currency into his map pocket and made for the steps.

There was another louder explosion much closer. It was followed by a cracking sound in the ceiling. Dust showered down.

'Come on. Shorty ... everybody ... quick ... come down here ... get back against the wall!'

Another colossal chunk of ceiling the size of a double-decker bus came careering down and landed on top of the vault, the throne and the area immediately behind the throne. The entire building moved as if it was an earthquake. The end wall wobbled momentarily then collapsed slowly from the bottom like a Fred Dibnah chimney. The wall adjoining followed, then the remainder of the beautiful arched roof fell in.

The black eastern sky looked evilly down on the surviving wall, the two arches and the piles of debris. The scene of devastation was illuminated in silhouette by yellow flames rising ever higher from the burning palace stables. A cloud of dust forty feet high swirled, rose up over the ruins and hovered there in the sweltering blackness for a few moments, then it fell, and momentarily, it seemed, there was a reverential silence.

T W O

---

*First-floor flat, Thirsk Road, Castlecombe, North Yorkshire, UK,
15 December 2003*

The music was loud. Very loud. It was a new CD from
The Boggs. It was four bars repeated and repeated and
repeated. It had shot straight to the top of the charts. Every
single record The Boggs released shot straight to the top.
They were the world's biggest-selling boy band. Seemingly,
millions adored the repetitive, incomprehensible lyrics delivered by the four red-throated teenagers. The racket emanated
from a new powerful ghetto-blaster in the first-floor flat
immediately above Mr and Mrs Carrington's confectionery
and bread shop on the main street in Castlecombe. That
evening, the ghetto-blaster was belting out at full volume, and
there was banging on the ceiling from the old lady in the flat
above, who applied her stick to the floor when her tolerance
level had been exceeded.

Unbeknown to the music lover, Ronald Kass, the door of
his flat was silently opened and an intruder tiptoed in.

Kass was a happy young man. He was sitting on the couch
eating his evening meal and intermittently accompanying
The Boggs by drumming with a fork on the wooden arm of

the settee. Suddenly, he spotted the intruder. There was a brief exchange of words. Something glinting and sharp caught the light, and there was a scuffle followed by a yell. Blood spurted on to the wooden floor; a trickle of red tracked across a floorboard.

The CD player went dead: so did Kass.

Castlecombe House Hotel, North Yorkshire, UK, 16 December 2003

'Same again, Mr Spence? Is it still white wine and lemonade, with ice?'

'Aye,' ex Detective Inspector Frank N. Spence said, pushing the empty glass across the bar towards the young man in the smart blue and black suit with the red dickie bow.

'How's the writing going, sir?' the young man said, trying to show an interest.

Spence pursed his lips. 'Slow, lad. Slow. *Very* slow.'

'Hmm. I hear they're going to make your book into a film, sir.'

Spence pursed his lips. 'That's what they say, lad, aye.'

The young man put a coaster with a rose motif on it in front of the big man. 'I read they've paid you a £100,000 for the film rights alone!' he said, his eyes glowing.

'Gross exaggeration, lad. Gross exaggeration.'

The barman looked disappointed. He thoughtfully placed the freshly filled glass on the coaster. Then he smiled. 'But you'll be doing all right, sir, I'll bet,' he said with a knowing nod. 'That'll be £2,50, please.'

Spence sniffed.

'Not as well as you're doing, lad, I think,' he said digging into his back pocket and peeling off a fiver from a thin bundle of notes.

He noticed a newspaper tucked between pump handles on top of the bar. He reached out towards it. The barman came back with the change.

'Borrow your paper?'

'Help yourself. It's *there* for customers, Mr Spence.'

It was the *North Eastern Record*, a local weekly. Spence opened it up. The headline read: *We've got him!* This was followed by eight pages about the American finding and capture of Saddam Hussein in an underground bunker on the outskirts of Baghdad.

Spence had already heard all about it. For the past two days, the television news had shown repeated pictures of the deposed ruler with a scruffy beard, being medically examined and having a torch shone into his mouth. Spence turned over the pages rapidly to see if there was anything else of interest. At the tail end of the article was a photograph showing the bombed ruins of the Glass Palace near Baghdad and a paragraph about millions of 100 dinar notes and a highly valuable jewelled Persian Salamander being lost in the disaster. There was a coloured photograph of the Salamander with big diamonds and rubies sparkling out of its lapis lazuli body.

Mr Hoffman, the hotel proprietor, put his nose round the door of the little bar. He was a very tall man with a big stomach, beard, smart double-breasted suit, monogrammed little finger ring and a continental accent. 'Ah, there you *are*, Mr Spence. And how's our author today? Is everythink satisfactory?'

Spence swivelled round on the stool.

'Yes, thank you.'

'Your vife's been on the phone. She vants that you should ring her back.'

Spence sighed, groaned and pulled a face like a man sucking a lemon he had thought was an orange.

'Did you tell her I was here?'

'No, sir, Mr Spence. Of course not,' he said with a big smile and he shot out through the doors as if he was on the end of a piece of elastic.

Spence turned back to the bar. He wrinkled his nose then rubbed his chin. He didn't want to phone his wife just yet. Rene would only yap at him. He'd left the house that morning to get away from interruptions, argument and controversy. He had not long since had a big success with a novel, his first, and was feverishly working on a follow-up. He liked to write in solitude in a little converted box room upstairs next to the bathroom, but sometimes his wife Irene would get a bee in her bonnet and keep popping in to say something about nothing. This morning had been like that. He'd get into the writing and imagine he really was in court or investigating a murder in some interesting – maybe exotic – place and then his wife would come barging in with some trivial tale or query, completely breaking the spell. When she'd gone, it'd take him five or ten minutes to work himself back into the story. This morning she had been in to chat three times in half an hour; he got so angry he came out. He'd had his hair cut and been to the bank and decided to pop in for a drink in his favourite drinking hole. Now she had tracked him down. He knew he would have to ring her back.

He closed up the newspaper, folded it, put it back between the pump handles, took a sip of the wine, grunted silently then reached into his pocket for his mobile phone. He tapped in the number and pressed the call button. It was answered almost immediately.

'You've had the damned thing switched off!' she began

without any preamble. 'Whatever for? How can I reach you when the damned thing is switched off? And where are you?'

'I'm in the park. Having a walk. Getting some exercise,' he lied, effortlessly. He knew she wouldn't believe him. It was his way of annoying her.

'You're a liar. I *know* you're at Castlecombe House. Mr Hoffman told me. I suppose you're getting quietly slewed.'

His mouth tightened. 'You know, Rene, you're enough to send a man to drink! Instead of rattling away running my battery down, you could tell me what you want me for. Are you desperate for my company for some particular reason? Or have you a mad, passionate desire to take me to bed to ravish me?'

'Huh!' she snapped indignantly 'Don't be so *ridiculous*! It's high time you got a *proper* job again, to straighten out your sick mind.'

'*What!*' he bawled. 'I've *got* a proper job. I'm a writer, for goodness' sake! I've written a bestseller! Some people seem to think that's pretty good for a fifty-year-old copper with only a secondary-school education … who's recovering from having a bullet in his belly. What's the matter with you? And why are you always checking up on me? Do you think I've got a fancy woman closeted away somewhere?'

'Huh!' she snapped, but she realized she was losing the argument. 'I was worried about you, you great lump. I don't know why. But you haven't been discharged from the doctor's long. And you *drink* too much. How are you going to get back?'

He hadn't a clue.

'I'll get back all right,' he asserted energetically.

'The post's come: I thought you'd want to know. You're always hovering by the front door these days, waiting for *something* important. There's the gas bill, one from the Inland Revenue and there's one from North Yorkshire Police postmarked Castlecombe.'

Spence blinked on hearing the last item. What would his local cop shop want to write to him about? The place where he had worked for more than twenty years. The place where he'd last done 'a proper job'. If it was some detail about a case or something, they could have phoned him. It would have been quicker and cheaper.

'All right,' he growled. 'I'll be back in about half an hour.'

'I might not be here,' she replied mischievously. Then she added, 'Look, if you're not fit, Frank, don't drive yourself back. Get a taxi.'

'I'm all right,' he lied.

The line went dead.

He cancelled the mobile and dropped it into his pocket.

He knew he'd have to get a taxi and come back for his car later.

He sniffed and looked up for the barman. He wasn't there. He couldn't see anybody through the half-door to the other bar or hear any sign of activity either. He swivelled round on the stool.

The only person in the room was an unsavoury young man who was always there, seated by the door at a little table, with a glass of some dark booze, which always seemed half full. The man was an incongruous limpet with a podgy face, thick lips that were always wet, and little eyes that slid around red pools. He looked as if he enjoyed petty crime and minor perversions. His wardrobe was typically sixties Oxfam, and when he wasn't staring out of the window hoping to catch sight of something feminine, frilly, fast and cheap, he was shoving an inhaler like a stick of chalk up his nose.

Their eyes met. It was churlish not to speak. 'Good morning, lad.'

'Good morning, Mr Spence,' the little oily man replied.

The ex-policeman's jaw dropped. He turned back. 'You know me?'

'Naw. Just heard your name ... around,' he mumbled awkwardly without looking up.

Spence could tell when a man was lying.

'My name's Mr Tripp.'

'Oh? Yes. Right.'

The door between the two bars closed. The young barman had returned.

'Another glass, Mr Spence?' he said with a smile.

'Ah! No, thank you. I want a taxi.'

'I got your letter, sir. It said you wanted to see me urgently,' Spence said. 'I came as soon as I could.'

The chief constable beamed across the big desk with a smile like the man on the Steradent poster. Spence looked back at him closely and rubbed his chin. The smile was as genuine as Paul Daniels' magic kettle.

'Yes, Frank. Very good of you to come so promptly. Take a seat.'

Spence blinked. The chief had called him 'Frank' and thanked him for coming! There was something not quite right. He was well aware that he wasn't a copper any more and that that *would* make a difference. Even so, this was not the style of the niggardly, bad-tempered monster he had got to know over the past ten years ... who had never addressed him by his first name! Something unusual was definitely going on. He wondered what was coming up next.

He tentatively eased himself down into the plush upholstered chair facing the desk.

'Haven't seen you since you were in hospital, Frank. Has that wound cleared up? Did they get *all* the ... lead out?'

'Yes, sir, eventually.'

'Good. Good. That must be six months now?'

'Almost twenty months, sir.'

'Really? Hmmm. Yes. And how are you passing the time? Of course, you've written a book, haven't you?'

'Yes, sir.'

'Hmmm. Saw you on television. What's it called again?'

'*Scatter My Ashes*.'

He sniffed. 'Oh yes. Doing well, is it?'

'Very well.'

'I must read it. Hmmm. And what are you doing now? Have you found a job?'

'I've got a job, sir. That is my job now. I'm *writing*.'

'Oh?' His eyebrows shot up. 'What? Another book?'

'Yes.'

'Oh. I thought ...' He rubbed his chin a few times. 'Aah. Oh. Well, now, you know that we cleared up the Thompson gang. Both brothers have gone down for a long time ... thanks to your investigations and labours in that direction and the deposition to Judge Abercrombie you made ... from your bed.'

Spence nodded.

'Superintendent Marriott wrapped it all up, so you've no worries in that regard. That's history. You can put that *right* behind you.' He nodded, shaking both chins, to emphasize the point. 'Now, I've asked you to come in to see me because I was concerned that that injury, the trauma, the time you had in hospital, your compulsory retirement, followed by a stretch of inactivity, might have had psychological repercussions, you know. And I wanted to be sure that as one of my men you weren't ...' He stopped speaking, looked directly into his face and rubbed his chin.

Spence peered across at him. 'That's very kind of you, sir.

26

But I'm not round the twist if that's what you were about to say.'

The chief pursed his lips and then turned it into a repeat of the Steradent smile.

'Ah, yes. Exactly! Good. Good.'

The chief reminded Spence of the picture of Nero he'd seen somewhere, playing the violin, just after he'd stabbed his wife and mother to death and displayed their entrails round the throne room of his palace in Rome.

'I was going on to say, Frank, that because of your medical history, it's not now, of course, possible, as you know, to employ you in the force in the *regular* way, but I could perhaps put some part-time work your way, if you wanted it. Sort of ... on a freelance basis. As you will know, it's quite within my remit to call you or anybody else in ... as needed ... on a consultancy basis ...'

'It sounds very good of him, Frank,' Irene said, walking into the sitting room with two beakers of tea. 'You always told me he was a *nasty*, devious man,' she added.

Frank N. Spence was sitting in an easy chair at the side of the fireplace. A fire roared up the chimney back.

'Yes, he is,' he said, holding out his hand.

Irene passed a beaker to him.

'Always got something sly going on ... Underhand, you said he was. What did you tell him, then?' she said, settling into the easy chair.

'Ta, love. I told him I would think about it. I mean, if I'm doing my old job chasing villains, I can't be doing my writing. I wouldn't have the time. And I mean writing isn't like doing a crossword or knitting. You can't just do a bit and then go out and track a criminal down, get the evidence, suss it out, bring him to court, get him sent down, then go straight back to writing your book and pick it up where you left off. You'd have to re-read what you've written. Get under the character's skin again ... go into the plot ... get back into the magic of the thing.'

'Hmmm,' she said, moving a strand of red hair back over her ear. 'Yes, but ... Look, Frank, let's face up to it. Let's be realistic. I don't want to be a wet blanket but supposing *Scatter My Ashes* is a fluke.'

His eyes flashed. He put the beaker down on a coaster on the library table.

'A fluke?' he said. He pursed his lips and shook his head.

'Well, it *is* your first novel. Supposing it's just a one-off. Say you've been lucky. I mean, it's a great read and it's well written, but they say there's a book in everyone. Maybe that was *your* one.'

'Aye. And it's on the bestseller lists. It's being reprinted at this very moment. The large-print rights have been sold. It's coming out in paperback. And there's that American company sniffing around for an option to make it into a film.'

'Yes. Yes. I know. And that's for *Scatter My Ashes*. It's a great plot. But you've always said the plot's the thing. Well, *that* plot is really all about the Thompson brothers' gang, isn't it? I mean, all right, you've changed their names and set it in Cornwall, but the story is all about them and their gang and how your hero unravelled their racket, exposed the murderer, brought them all to justice and got shot into the bargain.'

He pursed his lips, shrugged and grudgingly said, 'Well, yes.'

'Well, do you think you've got as good a plot again? Is the plot for your new book as good as *Scatter My Ashes*?'

He scratched his ear. 'Yes. Maybe not. Maybe it is. I'm not sure.'

'Well, Frank, if you *go* for this, you could write *some* days and do a bit for the force on a consultancy basis on others. Now that wouldn't be bad, would it?'

He looked Irene straight in the face. She had big, beautiful eyes. She could be very persuasive when she wanted to be.

She smiled and nodded. 'And you'd be a consultant,' she added. 'Sounds important.'

He stuck out his chest. 'Sounds like a doctor,' he said with a grin. Then he said, 'Hey! It'd look good on the dust jacket of my next book, wouldn't it? Consultant to Castlecombe Police ...'

'And if you do it, it would mean that you'd know what's going on, first hand. You'd be up to date with all the latest scams and rackets, the new technology, the forensics ... and it'd keep you going in realistic, authentic plots, wouldn't it?'

He nodded. 'Ah!' He licked his lips. He rubbed his chin. There was something in what she said.

'*And,*' she added with emphasis, 'you'd be bringing some money in, just in case *Scatter My Ashes* is a fluke.'

His eyes flashed.

'It's not a fluke!' he roared.

THREE

'Come in.'

Spence sighed.

The strident, uncouth voice of Haydn Marriott was unmistakable.

Spence squared his shoulders and purposefully pushed open the office door.

Marriott looked up slowly from his desk.

He had been detective superintendent at Castlecombe for the past eight years and had been Spence's immediate superior when he had had to leave the force twenty months earlier.

'Oh, it's you, lad,' he said with a sneer. He was a tall skinny man with receding hair, who never smiled and always looked in pain. Spence always said it was because his piles were being strangled by the string in his Y-fronts.

'Come in. Come in. Been expecting you. I knew it wouldn't take much to get you back on the money-grubbing trail. The chief said you'd leapt at the chance of earning a bit of extra brass. Hmm. I don't see why we don't shut a blind eye and employ you in the regular way. It'd be a damned sight cheaper than paying you out of the petty cash, but there it is. Well, sit down.'

Spence pulled up the chair by the desk.

'Thank you, sir.'

'We *could* manage, you know,' Marriott continued assertively. 'We're not on our backs quite yet. This isn't an absolute necessity. You could stop at home and carry on writing your ... penny dreadfuls or whatever it is. I'm quite sure we could at least maintain the same clear-up rate as last year without your invaluable help.'

Spence wasn't too pleased at the superintendent's commentary; he had expected to suffer *some* indignity at his hand, it was his way, but this sarcastic monologue was becoming insufferable. He didn't know it but he was getting dangerously near to having his mean little nose reddened.

'It's that the chief's got a phobia about our place in the clear-up rate chart,' Marriott continued, swivelling the chair round to him. 'Doesn't want us to be in the bottom twenty-five per cent.'

He sniffed and looked Spence up and down again.

'Well, now, how's your health?'

'I'm fine, sir.'

'Are we all healed up?'

'Yes.'

'I don't want you making any excuses and blaming it on the fact you've been shot in the gut. Everybody knows *all* about that. And you've had a good long rest and the appropriate compensation.'

Spence wrinkled his nose. He'd had a small lump sum, an increment added to his pension and the sack. He wasn't certain if it could be described as 'appropriate'.

'Well, mmm. You can use Asquith's office,' he continued. 'He's off with flu, as is my other DI, Cooke. They've been off sick for weeks. We are very greatly undermanned, lad, I have to tell you. That new strain of flu has a grip on it like Camilla. It's swept through this station faster than a teenager running up a phone bill. I've got four sergeants and a dozen or so constables off. There's a few DCs out on enquiries. Nobody on standby. The CID office is like the Cherie Blair fan club.'

He paused and sniffed noisily. He reached out for a file of papers in front of him. 'Better find you *something*, then.'

Spence nodded eagerly. Now to the nitty-gritty. 'I'll need a temporary ID card or something, won't I, sir?'

The superintendent dropped the file and pulled a disagreeable face, like Jacques Chirac sampling English wine at number ten.

'Oh no, lad. No. You're not a proper policeman. You're not *part* of the force; you'll be commissioned to do specific work *for* the force. You come under the category of casual or occasional labour, like a taxi driver, a window cleaner or someone we might set on to sterilize the telephones or unblock the lavatories.'

Spence breathed in deeply and out slowly. Then suddenly he said, 'Well, give me a case to work on, then. Let's get started.'

Marriott stared at him uncertainly for two seconds, and rubbed his chin.

'Aye. Right,' he said and put down the file. He reached forward across the desk to a wire basket. He picked out a telephone message sheet, glanced at it and then looked up.

'Here's something. Came in five minutes ago. A café in the town been broken into overnight. Owner arrived to find a window broken and the place in a mess. You can sort *that* out, for a start. It'll be a nice easy job for you to ease yourself back into *proper* work again. It'll not be too strenuous.'

Spence's jaw dropped. He snatched up the paper, glanced at it and frowned. 'A break-in?'

It was the sort of job you might give a PC to sort out on his first day. It was typical of the mean little man.

Without looking back, Spence made for the door.

'Not sure if anything was actually taken. I've already informed SOCO, so you needn't worry about that.'

'Right, sir,' Spence muttered through gritted teeth.

'Use Asquith's office. It's next to your old office.'

Spence closed the door quietly: he had wanted to slam it. He was relieved to get away from him. He had almost been at the point of telling him where to stuff the job. He made his way purposefully up the corridor and soon found the room with the words '*DI Alan Asquith*' painted in gold on the door. He had never heard of Asquith. He must have been a new lad. He turned the knob and pushed it open. He stood in the doorway of the tiny office and looked in. There was a desk with a telephone on it, a black leather swivel chair, green steel cupboard with a coat hook on the side, two visitors' chairs and the small table at the back. It was a replica of his old office. He smiled as he thought of times past.

A young woman's voice from behind startled him.

'Inspector Spence?'

He looked round.

'Yes. I suppose it is.'

A pretty, young policewoman in uniform smiled sweetly at him and said, 'Good morning, sir. I'm WPC Gold. The super has told me to report to you.'

Spence strode into the room and crossed to the swivel chair. 'Well, come in, lass, come in.' He turned back to face her, sniffed and said, 'Well, what is it that you have to report?'

'I'm to assist you, sir,' she said pertly.

Spence gawped at her. His eyes narrowed and he rubbed his chin.

She looked into his face and smiled. Her big eyes twinkled.

'You used to work here, sir, didn't you? You got shot by Rikki Thompson and then wrote a book about it, didn't you? I've seen you on television,' she gabbled.

'That was my father,' he lied. Then he sniffed and said, 'What's your name again, lass?'

'WPC Gold, sir,' she said. 'And I'm ever so pleased to be your assistant.'

'Well, hear this, WPC Gold. You might be on my team,' he said, stabbing the air with a finger, 'but you're not my assistant, not yet. I'll be having a sergeant … a *male* sergeant, to assist *me*.'

'But there aren't any sergeants available, sir. Male *or* female,' she added pointedly. 'They are all off with flu … or something.'

Spence's jaw tightened. He stared at her. She was very pretty and very smartly turned out. She smiled sweetly. He didn't smile back, he looked away for a moment and then back at her.

'I'll be having a DC then,' he said confidently.

'I don't think so, sir. As it is, the super's taken me off traffic. There really isn't anybody else,' she said evenly.

He didn't reply. His face said it all. Eventually, he threw up his hands, shook his head and dropped into the swivel chair.

She tentatively advanced towards him. 'I'm really very good, sir. I've passed *all* my exams. I was top in the intake,' she said quickly.

He gazed down at the desk top, shaking his head.

'How old are you?'

'Nineteen, sir,' she replied brightly.

He shook his head again. Several times. Then he looked up, his eyes staring.

'Nineteen?' he pondered. '*Nineteen!*' he suddenly bawled. Then he stood up.

'Yes, sir. My mother says I'm very mature for my years.'

'Oh, does she?' he grunted curtly. 'Nineteen. Do you know, WPC Gold, I've got stuff in my fridge at home older than you!'

Her jaw dropped.

The phone rang.

His eyebrows shot up. He looked down at the instrument on the desk and wrinkled his forehead. He hesitated then reached out and snatched it up.

'Spence,' he spat into the mouthpiece.

'Aye.'

It was Superintendent Marriott.

'Yes, sir.'

'There's another report of a break-in. It's at an ice-cream factory on the Durwood Estate. The Sunshine Ice-Cream Company. Add *that* to your list, and make your own arrangements with SOCO. It's *your* case.'

Spence wrinkled his nose. 'Right, sir.'

The earpiece clicked and the line went dead.

He replaced the phone, licked his lips and looked across at the young woman.

She smiled at him.

He didn't return the smile. He rubbed his hand across his mouth, blew out a long sigh then made a decision.

'Right, Constable Gold, let's get this show on the road.'

She grinned and turned towards the door.

FOUR

The sky was as grey as a judge's wig.

WPC Gold spotted the white SOCO transit van parked on the yellow line outside the small café on the main shopping street in the middle of Castlecombe. Spence pulled up behind, got out of the car and walked briskly down the side of it.

Gold came running up behind, and together they made their way purposefully across the shiny wet flagstones to the door of the tiny café. Spence remembered that the business had recently been a post office and newsagents. The post-office counter had been closed down and the owners had moved the much reduced business to smaller premises across the street.

Above the glass-panelled door was a sign that read '*Roy's Café*'. The door was ajar, and Spence noticed a pane, eight by ten inches, had been smashed; some shards of glass were on the step and on the mat inside. He sniffed and pointed to it.

'Here, lass. Make a note of it.'

Gold nodded and took out her notebook.

A young man in white paper overalls, white hat and pink boots came out of the café. They exchanged glances.

The man recognized him, smiled broadly and said, 'Hello, sir. What *you* doing here? I thought you were too badly injured to come back to work. I'd heard you'd retired.'

'No. No,' Spence said. Then, without any expression, he added, 'I died.'

The young man grinned.

'I read your book, sir. Great stuff,' he said as he pulled off the white headcover.

Spence nodded his thanks.

Gold chimed in. 'The inspector's helping us out with some cases, Ron.'

Spence stared at her, blinked then turned back to the young man. 'Aye, lad. What you got?'

The young man smiled at her and then at him.

'Nothing much. Looks like an intruder, or intruders. The owner says he can't see anything taken. There's quite a mess in there. Paper sacks ripped open ... sugar spread about.'

'Any dabs, footprints ...'

'No fingerprints. Got a footprint, though.'

Spence's eyebrows shot up.

'Nothing else, sir.'

'Who reported it?'

'The owner. Roy Cattermole, sir. About 8.30 this morning. Came to open up.'

Gold glanced up from her note-taking.

'Do you know where he is now, Ron?'

'Was around here. Sat in a car. Waiting. Somewhere.'

Spence said, 'Right, lad. Ta. Let me know about the footprint, SAP.'

'Of course.' The DC turned away then turned back. 'Nice to have you back, sir,' he said as he unzipped the front of the overall to remove it.

Spence smiled. The welcome was unexpected. He was surprised and shook his head.

'Thanks,' he said. 'Hey. There's another call come in. Will you pick that up next?'

'Will you ask the boss, sir? She's just coming out now.'

Spence's eyebrows shot up. He didn't expect the head of Castlecombe forensics to be female. He thought that was a novelty exclusive to TV cop shows.

The young man moved away and opened the sliding door of the van.

A tall slim woman in a white overall, white hat and pink boots came out of the shop carrying a plastic holdall. She looked at the WPC and then at Spence and said, 'Who's this?'

Gold stepped forward. 'This is Inspector Spence, ma'am.'

'Oh yes, the writer,' she said with a wry smile. She pulled back the hat and shook her hair free.

Spence looked into her well-lined, handsome face and wrinkled his nose.

'Today, missus, I'm just a copper. Who are you?'

'Dr Chester. I'm head of forensics at Castlecombe.'

He blinked. Things had certainly changed in twenty months. 'Oh,' he said. 'Right.' He licked his lips and frowned.

'I'm only out of the lab today to speed things up. We're finished here,' she said, placing the holdall in the van and jumping in beside it.

'Yes. Right. So your lad was saying.' Spence rubbed his chin with a hand. 'There's a call come in from The Sunshine Ice-Cream Company on the Durwood Estate. Looks like another break-in. Can you pick that up now?'

'Don't see why not, Inspector,' she called out as she slammed the door.

He watched the van pull away from the kerb and rubbed his chin again.

'Ta,' he murmured pointlessly.

Gold said, 'That's good of her, sir, isn't it?'

He shrugged his shoulders. 'It's only round the corner.'

She looked at him slyly and smiled.

A middle-aged man and a woman bustled up to them.

'Are you in charge?' the man said to Spence. 'Have they finished in there?'

'Are you the owner, sir?' asked Spence.

He nodded. 'I'm Roy Cattermole and this is my wife. Do you think you'll find who's done it?'

'Don't know, Mr Cattermole. Don't know yet. What exactly is missing?'

'Haven't really had chance to look. There's no money in there or anything like that.'

'Hmmm. Well, wait here a minute with my WPC, will you?'

'I got to get ready for my customers,' he pleaded.

'It's a mess in there,' his wife added. 'Got to get it cleaned up.'

'Aye. I'll just have a quick look round,' Spence said with a smile and dashed through the door.

The café comprised one room with two main areas divided by a counter. The area nearest the door had a dozen or so tiny tables with chairs around them, most of which were covered in white powder, like a winter scene. It seemed to have been sprayed around indiscriminately. He looked at it, dabbed his finger on the table tops and confirmed that it was sugar. The part-emptied large paper sacks that had contained the stuff were dropped randomly on the floor. The stainless-steel counter in the middle of the room had a cash till on it with the drawer open, showing it to be empty. Behind it were the preparing, storing and cooking areas comprising two domestic ovens, a fridge, a sink, worktops, shelves with pots, food store, pans and cutlery. There were big windows on two walls that could not be opened. They had two extractor fans built into the glass. The big windows made the little café seem airy and bright. There was no other entrance to the premises.

Two minutes later, Spence came out on to the pavement.

Mr and Mrs Cattermole rushed up to him.

'Can we go in now?'

He looked at them and pointed with his thumb.

'Yes. Thank you,' he said. 'It's all yours.'

They rushed past him to the door.

He called after them: 'Find out what's been taken, will you?' He turned to Gold. 'You'd better go in there with them. See what's missing. Don't be long.'

She nodded.

He pursed his lips as he watched her pick her way across the pavement, between the shoppers, and then go through the door into the café. He ambled across to the car and stood by the door. He massaged his ear lobe between finger and thumb and gazed down the busy street. He was wondering why intruders would want to spread sugar around. They clearly didn't want to *steal* the stuff, they seemed merely to want to throw it around. Yet there were plenty of brightly coloured, sticky substances that would have made a far more sensational mess and work for others to clear up – eggs, tomatoes, jam, honey, milk. And there were plenty of pots to break. It would be hard to believe the intruders were vandals. They were not the usual young thieves, looking for drug money. Young men of a certain type would not have been able to resist lifting one or more of the vicious-looking carving knives he had noticed in the block on a worktop. He sighed. This was one of those posers that, from now on, would bother him when his mind wasn't engaged on something more demanding. It would flood his thoughts during boring interludes while watching television at night or shaving in the morning. Hmmm.

A clock chimed.

He heard it and looked around. It was the town hall clock. It was half-past ten. Then, behind him, in the entrance to a ginnel, he noticed an old man with a greying beard seated on something hidden by a sack, which also covered his knees. He was wearing sunglasses, a thick black coat, scarf and woollen maroon stocking hat. He sat in silence, his big bony head slowly moving to his extreme right, holding it there briefly, then returning to his extreme left and repeating the motion as though scanning the area in front of him. At his feet was a small pile of Christmas trees with a crudely hand-drawn sign that simply read: '£5 *each*'.

Spence grinned and ambled over to him.

'Now then, Zack, what you doing out here? You'll catch your death of cold.'

The old man's head stopped the scanning action. He looked up, and his mouth opened, but he didn't speak.

'Don't you know me?' Spence called cheerily.

The man smiled and his mouth suddenly twitched twice to one side.

'Course I knows you, Inspector,' he said in a broad Dublin accent. 'Keep down your voice, wilt cher? You'll ruin my business. I tort you'd gone to glory. Then I heard you'd done a James Joyce and were in the money. Now you must be back on the sniff again.'

'I am. I am. Haven't seen you in a long time.'

'Please don't hang around me here. You'll take all the trade away and ruin my reputation, Inspector. Oi'll be in the Fat Duck for a jar at twelve o' clock, if you care to join me.'

Spence whispered, 'I'll be there,' then he straightened up and in a normal voice said, 'You can't stay here, sir. Move along. Come on, now. Move along.'

He turned away and made for the car.

Zack's mouth twitched twice but no other part of him moved.

Gold saw the tail end of the exchange between the two men as she came out of the café and made for the car. She took hold of the car door handle, looked back at the old man thoughtfully and then at Spence.

'He's not packing up. He's not moving. Do you want *me* to move him along, sir?'

'No,' Spence said, lowering himself into the driving seat.

'He's a tramp, sir. He's a beggar,' she said irritably.

Spence's jaw stiffened. He shook his head.

'He's not a beggar. He's selling Christmas trees.'

'I've seen him before. He's an unlicensed vendor, sir. He should be moved on.'

Spence's eyes flashed. 'Get in the car,' he said angrily.

'But, sir …'

'Get in the car *and shut up*,' he snapped.

Gold's eyes flashed. Her mouth dropped open. She looked worried. She got in the car, closed the door and dived for her seatbelt. She avoided his eyes.

Spence let in the clutch and pulled into the traffic. It was a full thirty seconds before he spoke.

'Didn't they teach you anything about discipline at Hendon? I thought you said you were top of your intake?'

There was a pause. She shook her head.

'I shouldn't have argued, sir. I know. And I'm sorry,' she said without looking up.

Spence pursed his lips as he drove silently out of the main street towards the Durwood Estate. When they were on the Darlington Road, he breathed out noisily and shook his head.

'Firstly, he's one of the best snouts I have ever had. He bends the law but he isn't dishonest. So I turn a blind eye to

43

trivial things. I shouldn't, but I do in *his* case, because it pays me to. I need him more than he needs me. Also, unusually, I have a soft spot for him. He's disadvantaged in several ways. He's had little or no education, he's old and he's almost blind. If ever you see him in the street or anywhere, in the future, walk on by. Pretend you haven't seen him. You'll be doing yourself a favour.'

She didn't reply immediately. Then she nodded and said, 'Right, sir.'

'Secondly, you don't seem to have grasped the merit of discipline. It's not one-sided, you know. It's very simple. If your superior gives you an order, then to all intents and purposes, that order is good, valid, correct, appropriate and intelligent. If subsequently the order is shown *not* to be all or any of those, and you have taken some action, given some evidence or made some declaration or decision *based* upon that order, and you land in trouble, your defence is that your superior said it, and that as he's your superior, you took it to be correct. The courts and any fair-minded person would recognize what you say to be right and ergo, you would get off scot-free. Your superior, on the other hand, would be seen to be the idiot he is, be appropriately reprimanded and punished, *not you*. Understand?'

'Yes, sir.'

'Now if you feel the need to question something I say or do in the future ...' He rubbed his chin slowly and then went on. 'I don't want to quench your natural curiosity and make you into an automaton ... but pick a quiet, sensible time, *after the event*, and ask me. And unless you have wound me up and got me rattled beyond all reason, I'll try and talk to you sensibly, soberly and reasonably about it. Right?'

'Yes, sir.'

'And one last thing, while my blood is up. When I am

talking to somebody, don't interrupt and try to take the conversation over from me.'

Her eyes flashed and she exhaled noisily.

'Anything else?'

'Yes. Don't sulk! That's what kids do!'

There was a pause while Spence drove into the Durwood Estate and stopped to look up at the signpost for The Sunshine Ice-Cream Company. He spotted it and let in the clutch.

'Now what did you find out in the café?'

There was the slightest suggestion of a sniff. 'Mr Cattermole said that there's nothing taken that he could see, sir.'

Spence wrinkled his nose. 'Mmmm.'

He drove down the quiet road of the new red-brick estate, past small factories and warehouses, looking for the ice-cream factory.

Gold breathed in and out a few times in a controlled way. She knew what Spence had said was right. She licked her lips and gradually cooled down. Then she said, 'Must be kids having a lark, sir. Probably high on drugs or booze.'

'It's not kids,' he said, seeing the factory ahead. 'Kids would have made a much bigger mess than that. And they would have enjoyed tipping out *all* the contents of the sacks; emptying out the last bit in the bottom and discarding the sack. The emptying out and throwing away the sack would have provided kids with the *most* fun. The sacks weren't emptied out, and there were whole sacks of flour and raisins untouched. No. Hmmm. There was a reason for spraying that sugar around. I'll be damned if I can understand it, though.'

Gold's eyes opened wider. He was right, of course. She wondered why she hadn't reasoned it out like that.

'There was a footprint as well,' he added. 'I expect it'll be a man's.'

She made a mental note to check out if he was right about that as well.

On the left a bright red and orange sign on a white board told them they had arrived outside The Sunshine Ice-Cream Company. He turned off the service road and drove the car up to the modern-brick built building and parked next to the SOCO van on the front.

There was a door marked 'Reception'. Spence pressed down the handle and walked in. Gold followed. It was a tiny room with a table, a chair and a phone. A young woman in a white coat came in through the door opposite. She spotted the WPC's uniform.

'There's police already here,' she said.

'Aye,' Spence said, 'smiling, we're the important ones.'

She didn't smile back.

'I'll tell Jack,' she said and went out.

Almost immediately, Dr Chester and the young DC, Ron Todd, came through the door in their white paper overalls. She smiled at Spence.

'Ah. There's nothing here for us, Inspector,' she said. 'Access and egress by pressure to a side door. Ingredients store ransacked. Minimal disturbance elsewhere. Might be ritualistic; if it is, I don't understand it. No fingerprints, footprints, DNA or anything else. Intruder appears to have been wearing leather, plastic or rubber gloves. I think that's about it. It's all yours. Must dash.'

'Oh? Ta, Doc. Be in touch.'

The SOCOs left through the outside door.

A big man all in white and wearing a cream straw hat came in from the factory. 'More police?'

'Just need to see where the intruder has been, sir. And the site of the disturbance. Are you the proprietor?'

'Yes. Jack Mantalini. Come in. It's a peanut job, this. Just telling your associates, nothing has been taken. It's silly. We wouldn't leave money here. It's out of season anyway. Nobody in their right mind would rob an ice-cream factory in December.' He pulled a face. 'It will cost me nigh on a thousand pounds, though,' he added gruffly.

'Hmmm,' Spence grunted sympathetically. 'How did the intruder get in?'

'Forced the side door. I'll show you. Follow me.'

He moved rapidly through the small factory, past machines and vats interconnected with stainless-steel pipes. Spence and Gold followed. There didn't seem to be any staff around and no production was in progress. From another part of the building, a compressor started up, rattled its safety guards and then began a regular gentle hammering. He led them through a door into the garage, where two vans were parked, down a short passageway past two doors marked Ladies and Gents, to a small door at the end. He reached out and opened it. It led outside. He pointed to the lock. It was not very substantial, and was hanging off the white painted door.

'Found it like that this morning.'

Spence sniffed and said, 'Brute strength. Just heaved himself or themselves against it.'

Mantalini nodded.

'Whereabouts in the building have they been?'

'Just the room where we store the ingredients, I think. Nothing else was disturbed. They might have had a look round.'

'Can we see?'

He tramped back into the garage past the back of the vans again to another door.

'It's very messy.' He turned the doorknob, pushed the door open and switched on the light.

It was like looking into an igloo. It was white everywhere, like a fresh fall of snow, over racks and shelves of boxes, cases and carboys.

'The white powder,' Spence said, 'what is it?'

'Sugar,' Mantalini said. 'It was in paper sacks. Fifty kilos per sack. Twenty sacks of sugar.'

'Every sack opened?'

'Yes. What for? God knows.'

'What about other ingredients?'

'Not touched. There's all sorts in there. Flavourings, colourings, chocolate, gelatine, ice-cream powder, dried milk. There's margarine in the fridge.'

'But only the sugar interfered with?'

'Yes.'

'The other stuff is not in sacks?'

'No. What's that got to do with it?'

'Would they be in the dark? Do you switch the juice off at the main when you leave at night?'

'Yes. Why? Wouldn't a burglar bring his own torch?'

'You'd think so. Do you usually have as much stock of sugar out of season?'

'This isn't a lot, really, and it's cheaper to buy out of season. This sugar was only delivered yesterday.'

Spence pursed his lips, then turned to Gold. 'Hear that, lass?' He stared at her and frowned. 'Are you getting all this down?'

She bristled.

'Yes, sir,' she replied and stabbed the ballpoint hard in the notebook. She couldn't see why it might matter *when* the sugar was delivered. She couldn't see why it mattered whether the intruder brought a torch or not. A burglar worthy of the name would bring a torch, wouldn't he? And why would he highlight the point that the burglar might only be interested in stuff in sacks? She had written all the questions and answers down but she couldn't see the point in it all.

'I think that's all for now, sir. If you think of anything else, give me a ring at the station.'

Mantalini said, 'Do you think they'll be back?'

Spence pursed his lips.

'No. But you could do with a stronger lock on that side door.'

Mantalini nodded.

'Are you going to be able to catch them, Inspector? Or is all this just a waste of time?'

Spence slowly shook his head.

'Oh no, sir. In *this* case, I can confidently say that we *will* … eventually.'

He suddenly looked at his watch. It was 11.52. Perfect timing. He had an appointment at the Fat Duck.

'Thank you for your help, and I am sorry you were pestered in this way.'

Mantalini appreciated the inspector's comment.

Spence took his leave and Mantalini saw them off through the reception door.

When they were in the car, Gold said, 'Do you really think we can catch the intruder, sir? Or were you just pacifying Mr Mantalini?'

'Oh no, lass. Oh no. We'll eventually catch this sweet-toothed nuisance. We'll catch him because, in this instance, his motive is so unusual. There'll be a simple answer, we just need a hint. It may take a bit of time, but we'll get him.'

'How do you know it's a him and not a her?'

'I don't. It's a matter of probabilities. I don't think a woman could easily move sacks of sugar weighing a hundredweight about the place. SOCO will have a man's footprint from the café job. Both jobs were done by the same person. If it was a man, I would say he's over thirty years of age, and he probably has *not* got a record.'

Her mouth dropped open.

'How do you know all that, sir?'

'He has no fascination for knives. He's mature. He doesn't break in with a jemmy or other conventional housebreaking tools. He is single-minded. He isn't interested in anything other than sugar. He's not looking for anything to steal. And he's not even stealing sugar … he's messing about with it. He may have a fetish: he may be ill. I want you to phone round the local forces. Start with North Yorkshire, South Yorkshire, Lincolnshire and so on and see if you can find any recent cases similar to these two. Same MO … You know, premises broken into, minimal disturbance, nothing stolen, sugar spread about the place …'

FIVE

'A pint of Guinness, a half of Old Peculier and two meat pies. There you are, Mr Spence. Help yourself to black pudding. There's a fork on the side. And there's your change. And congratulations,' the landlord said.

'Ta. Congratulations? What for?'

'Well, catching that gang, stopping a bullet, writing a book and getting your old job back.'

He smiled. 'I haven't got my old job back.'

'Oh. Sorry. Thought you had. I'll send it across. Where are you sat?'

'In the corner, t'other side of the fire. I'll take the drinks,' he said, picking up the glasses.

'Right,' the landlord said, putting the pies and cutlery on a tray. 'But you're back with the force, aren't you?'

'Sort of.'

'Ah. Well, I'll be seeing you tonight then.'

Spence hesitated. 'What? No. I don't think so.'

'I thought you'd be coming. I'm *sure* you're included.'

'What's this? What's happening then?'

'Haven't you heard? You remember Wally Walpole?'

'Aye. What about him?'

'He died. Last month.'

Spence's eyebrows shot up. He pursed his lips and shook

his head. 'Oh,' he said softly. He was saddened to hear of the early death of an old mate and friend. Wally Walpole had been on the force at Castlecombe for more than twenty years. He was a sergeant for the last four. When his wife died a few years back, he had retired from the force and emigrated to Australia to be near his son. Spence had liked Wally. He considered him to be the salt of the earth, everybody's friend. Not really dedicated enough to be a serious copper, but a good mate and great company on a long night's shift or a tedious observation job.

'What happened? He'd only be in his fifties.'

'Don't know. Everybody is gathering here tonight to have a drink to remember him.'

'What time?'

'5.30.'

'I'll be here.'

He picked up the two glasses, crossed the busy saloon bar, lowered his head under a beam, and stepped over the bench seat to reach the chair between the wall and the table in the corner. He placed the Guinness carefully on the table in front of Zack and sat down with his back to the wall.

'Thank you. It's nice to have you back, Mr Spence. Yes, that it is,' Zack said.

A pretty girl brought the tray with the pies, serviettes and knives across and placed them in front of them.

'Thanks, love.'

She smiled and left.

'Shall I cut up your pie, Zack?'

'If you please. Where's my glass?' he said, his hand expertly traversing the space on the table in front of him.

'You're getting there.'

He found it and cupped it securely.

'Ah.'

Spence watched him and smiled.

He took a sip, followed by a swig and put the glass carefully in front of him.

'I'm worried about the Weasel, Mr Spence,' Zack said, wiping cream foam off his lip with the back of his hand.

The Weasel was a well-known inveterate small-time crook: a multi-talented pickpocket, sneak thief and housebreaker. The Castlecombe force seemed to have been arresting him ever since time began. Spence had locked him up times without number in his early days on the beat. The man never learned. His name was Benny Teazel but was called the Weasel because of his little eyes, sharp nose and whiskery face.

Spence pushed the prepared pie in front of him. 'Aye, what about him?'

'He's been missing a week or more now. I have £60 of his, come up on a nag. He wouldn't be leaving me alone with his winnings all this time if he was all right. I knows that. I have asked around: nobody's seen him. I had thought he might have turned up today, but he's nowhere to be seen. I am getting worried, I can tell you. He's either unable to get here, or he's deliberately keeping out of the way.'

'I've heard nothing,' Spence said. 'I'll make enquiries.'

'I tink I should tell you sometink in confidence, like.'

Spence rubbed his hand across his mouth. 'Aye?'

'In confidence now, Mr Spence.'

'You know me, Zack.'

'Well, the Weasel told me, he was on a job ... he got a tip ... he was going to scratch round the visitors' bedrooms up at that posh hotel, Castlecombe House. He'd been touching up a filly what does some cleaning up there. She'd let him dummy up her pass key and when all the runners was supposed to be into their fodder, he was going to do a rummage round their rooms. He'd only just got started in the first room when he heard a voice on the landing and a rattle of keys. He doused the light and dived under a bed. Two men came in. They settled down, talking and drinking … very amical, loike. One was sat on the bed, the udder on a chair. He said they were talking about something called a Persian Salamander, he tort it was, and that it was something somebody else would give his right arm for, but even so, they got to arguing and one man said he would have to show it to somebody first. The other man said the money was not enough, that it was hidden in a safe place where nobody would ever find it, and that if he told anybody, he would split his gizzard. The Weasel said he tort he produced a carver at this point, and his blood ran cold. Anyhow, the man backed down, then the phone rang. Someone had come and one of them had to meet a man somewhere, so they left. The Weasel said he was so relieved, and didn't fancy doing *that* room any more. He gave them time to get well clear, then listened at the door and let himself out. As he closed it, three men come round the corner and see him. One says "what are you doing in there?" and starts singing out. The Weasel is naturally scared. He starts to run away down the corridor like it's the straight at Haydock Park. They start running after him, only three lengths behind and breathing heavy. He races round the landing, through a door or sometink, down some backstairs, tru the kitchen and away. Nobody can gallop faster than the Weasel, especially when he's scared. He said he ran all the way to the main road, and down the hill to the traffic lights before he stopped for breath. He was leaning against a telegraph pole when he saw a 4 x 4 roaring down the straight, behind him. Two men were hanging off their saddles, through the windows scouting round. He took a dive under a hawthorn bush and galloped his way towards the canal. He said he was glad to get away with his loife.'

Spence frowned and sighed.

'Where does the Weasel live these days?'

'He was lodging with an overweight filly what works in the butcher's on Ravenscar Road. She hasn't seen him for a week. I been to see her. She's got the hots for him. She's pulling her hair out. He owes her rent money, but she says if I see him to tell him that don't matter. Crazy woman!'

'No description of the men?'

'No. But they must be well shod and wrapped. Must have had a few quid in their pockets, lodging at Castlecombe House. What do you tink, Mr Spence? What do you tink?'

Spence pursed his lips and rubbed his chin.

'What's the name of the girl in the butcher's?'

'Gloria something, Mr Spence. There's only one lass in there.'

'I'll see what I can do, Zack.'

The Irishman shook his head.

'Tank you. And Mr Spence?'

'Yes?'

Zack grabbed the inspector's sleeve, leaned over close to him and whispered, 'And what in the name of Ian Paisley is a Persian Salamander?'

Spence tapped the left indicator and turned the car into New Street. A hundred yards ahead on the left-hand side was the police station. WPC Gold was standing in front of the main door looking at her watch. He knew he wasn't late: there were still a few seconds before two o'clock. As he got nearer, her face lit up. She sighed and smiled.

He stopped right in front of her and she leaned forward and opened the car door.

'*There* you are, sir,' she said brightly as she bounced into the seat and reached for the seatbelt.

Spence wrinkled his nose as he let in the clutch.

'I've got some news,' she said with a big smile.

'Oh yes?' Spence said, as he turned left towards the town centre. He sniffed. 'I hope it's *good* news, lass. I don't want any bad.'

Her eyes shone.

'Oh, it is, sir. It is,' she said, nodding her head several times. 'I made enquiries from North Yorkshire police and they've had four cases of breaking and entering and sugar spread about the place and so on, just like the two we've been looking into this morning. Two were in Harrogate, two in Skipton, and one was a school!'

Spence's pulse accelerated.

'Hmm,' he grunted. He licked his lips as he changed gear. 'And when did these break-ins occur?'

'Last night, sir.'

'Hmmm. He must be working overtime. Or is there more than one person? Any forensic? Any names?'

'No. Not as yet, sir. They are as confused as we are.'

Spence blinked, pursed his lips and was silent momentarily, then he said: 'I am *not* confused, lass. I can't as yet explain the phenomenon, but I am *not* confused. There will be a perfectly logical explanation for this sugar ... fetish, or whatever it is. It just needs winkling out, that's all.'

She tried to stifle a smile.

Spence didn't see her; he was looking at the road ahead and thinking.

The speed of the car increased as he reached the open dual carriageway, then suddenly he said, 'I want a map marked up to show where the break-ins have occurred. I want to see what pattern it makes.'

The roundabout that divided traffic for the A1, Middlesbrough and the holiday coast was coming up ahead. Spence pursed his lips. He didn't slow down. Instead, he drove all the way round it at the same speed, causing the tyres to squeal and Gold to sway inelegantly to the door, across the gear-change cover and then back against the door again as he steered the car through 360 degrees and then straightened up.

'I am taking you back to the station to get on with it. You can set it up in my office. I'll be in shortly. I've got a call to make. I'll give you my mobile number.'

He dropped Gold back at the station and five minutes later was on Ravenscar Road looking for the butcher's shop. It wasn't difficult to find. It was a smart, well-laid-out establishment on a small frontage of shops. He seemed to have chosen a quiet time. He went up the step and through the open door, coming face to face with a skinny man and a big woman dressed in white and navy blue.

When Spence saw the woman he blinked. She *was* a big lass … Handsome enough, he thought. Aged about thirty, with enough up front to suckle Yorkshire.

Her boss allowed them to talk privately in the white-painted preparation room at the back of the shop.

'It's Gloria, isn't it?'

'Yes,' she said in a quiet voice, looking down at the sawdust.

'Well, Gloria, my name is Spence, I'm a friend of Zack, and I'm making enquiries about Benny Teazel. And I understand you are a friend of his … that he lodges with you. Is that correct?'

She licked her generous lips then nodded.

'You're a policeman, aren't you, Mr Spence?'

'Well, sort of, but Zack is holding some money for him

and he'd like to give it to him, but Benny seems to have disappeared. Do you know where he is?'

Her face began to crease up. She was about to cry. She dragged up the corner of her white apron and put it to her eyes.

Spence licked his lips. He couldn't cope with crying women.

'What's the matter, Gloria? What is it?'

She breathed in deeply and looked up into his face.

'I don't know *where* he is, Mr Spence. I am very worried about him. He's been missing eight days now.'

Spence rubbed his chin. 'Well, when did you last see him?'

She sniffed. 'He had his tea at six o'clock a week last Tuesday, then said he was going out to the Fat Duck. I wanted to go with him but he said it was business. I haven't seen or heard from him since.'

There were more tears.

'He has a room in your house?'

'Well, yes.'

'Are all his clothes and things still there?'

'Yes.'

'Well, he'll be back then, won't he?' Spence said with a smile.

She looked up and, still wiping her eyes, said, 'Do you think so, Mr Spence? Do you really think so?'

Spence tried to look cheerful. 'Why not?' He beamed and patted her on the arm.

Gloria shook her head and blew her nose.

'Suddenly everybody wants to give him money,' she said. 'And he was always skint! There was a man here yesterday said he had a business proposition for him that would earn him a thousand pounds. A thousand pounds! It didn't sound right, Mr Spence. And he got ever so shirty when I told him

I still didn't know where he was. He didn't believe me and he shouted at me ... something nasty. His cold blue eyes stared right through me. It frightened me and it didn't sound right at all.'

Spence blew out a sigh. He agreed, it didn't sound right, but he didn't say so.

'What was this man like?'

'Ordinary, you know. He was tall, smart, bossy. He'd be about forty.'

Spence rubbed the lobe of his ear between finger and thumb. 'I don't think he'll come back, Gloria, but if he does, give me a ring at the station.'

Gloria's lowered eyes moved slowly from side to side.

'Do you think Benny's in some sort of trouble?'

He tried to smile. 'I'm sure it's nothing he can't handle,' he lied.

Gloria was smarter than she looked. Her lip quivered. 'Oh dear. I'm frightened, Mr Spence.'

'Not to worry,' he said. He went to pat her reassuringly on the elbow, and noticed her big arms had turned to goose-flesh.

It was 5.30 p.m.

WPC Gold lowered her head under the oak beam, placed two drinks on the table and shuffled on to the bench seat between Spence and another policeman. She had changed into street clothes and was now wearing a smart fitted coat and skirt.

'Ta, lass.'

The little bar in the Fat Duck was full to bursting with familiar faces from the station, which was only two streets away. They were mostly men, now out of uniform, and except for the fact that they were all tall and big, you might not realize they were policemen. Several cheery faces had been across to exchange a word of welcome and greeting with Spence and taken the opportunity to get to know pretty WPC Gold that bit better.

Everybody was chattering when Simon Dickenson stepped into the throng. He put his glass on the bar and stood with his back to it.

'Thank you,' he bawled loudly. 'Thank you, everybody. It's gone 5.30. Can I have your attention, please?'

The chattering ceased.

'Thank you. As chairman of the constables' branch of the federation, I call this extraordinary general meeting to order. Glad that so many could come. In view of the fact the booze is paid for, perhaps that's not surprising. We have a non-member present ... DI Frank N. Spence. He's here at the committee's invitation. I take it there are no objections?'

'No! No!' came enthusiastic mutters from round the little bar room.

'Right. And by the by, I will take this opportunity, on behalf of us all, to welcome him back into the force, particularly after what he went through two years ago at the hands of Rikki Thompson and er ... well, anyway ... And we also congratulate him on becoming an author. It's not often we get a real-life celebrity in our midst. Might be going to Hollywood soon, eh, Inspector? Anyway, you all know why we are here – it's to remember our dear friend and colleague, the late Wally Walpole.'

There were mutters of 'Yes,' 'Hear hear,' and 'Good old Wally'. Some held up their glasses.

Simon Dickenson put his hand into his pocket and pulled out an envelope.

'On Monday I got this letter from his son, which I propose to read out. It's from Bang Bang, near Darwin,

Northern Territory, Australia. And it's dated November 30th. It says:

"'Dear Mr Chairman, I regrettably have to tell you that my father, Walter Walpole, sadly died in a tragic fishing accident in the Indian Ocean on November 20th.'"

There were lots of sympathetic groans.

'Ah. Poor old Wally.'

Dickenson put up a hand to regain silence and their attention, and continued reading: "'Although he had officially retired, after Mum died he remarried a lady from Hawaii, called Marmalade Mary, and they had bought a curry stall, specializing in curried haddock, on the beach here at Bang Bang. He went into Darwin every day to buy fish in the pick-up. On this day, he got back to the beach, kicked off his flip-flops, took the box of haddock out of the back of the pick-up and was going to the bar door when he trod on a dispenser bottle of ketchup sticking out of the sand. He fell and hit his head – a real beaut – on a case of lager. He dropped the box of haddock and it split open and the fish and ice went all over him and on to the sand. Tragically, he didn't recover. (We had to throw most of the haddock away.) We had a proper preacher man come down from Darwin to do the necessary, and he is nicely buried quite close to the curry bar so that Marmalade Mary can keep an eye on him.

"'Of course, we are all devastated and I have to fetch the haddock now each day myself.

"'Dad always said to send £100 for all at Castlecombe nick to have a drink on him. So enclosed is £50 on account of things being a bit expensive just now. (The four handles alone cost £18 wholesale, to give you some idea. And my wife is expecting our sixth little joey in a fortnight.)

"'Hope you have a good drink on him. Dad would have liked to be there.

"'Yours faithfully,

"'Eric Walpole.'"

Simon Dickenson solemnly folded up the letter and put it back in his pocket.

There were a few sighs and groans.

'Thank you very much,' he said and turned back to the bar to collect his glass. Then he turned back quickly. 'Oh yes. The landlord tells me the money is now all spent. New orders now will have to be paid for. Thank you very much. That's all. Please carry on.'

There was a few seconds' silence and then everybody began to talk at once.

Gold said, 'You must have known Sergeant Walpole well, didn't you, sir?'

Spence nodded.

'Very well. We did a lot of nights as PCs together. And later on, many an obbo. Funny he should go out like that. He used to talk a lot about what he'd do when he got his wings ... That's what he used to say; that's the way he put it.'

'Oh?' she said. 'Was he religious then?'

'No ... no ... wouldn't say that. Although he was devil-may-care, he did talk a lot about death and the afterlife in a semi-serious way. I remember he said that it must take three days to reach heaven from earth, because Jesus came back from the dead in three days. And he used to say when you'd got your wings, it must be possible to travel round the world in virtually no time at all.'

Gold smiled politely and took a sip from her glass.

There was a pause.

Spence chuckled.

'I remember he said how when he died, he'd like to come back ... in spirit, I suppose you'd say ... and help us solve our backlist of unsolved crimes.'

Gold smiled. 'So he could be here, seeing and listening to us now, and presumably having a jolly good laugh at us? Or in Australia, checking on what his wife Marmalade Mary – what a funny name – was up to. Whether she was currying the haddock properly ...'

Spence smiled. He considered what curried haddock must taste like.

Gold thought about it for a second.

'He'd have a terrific advantage, wouldn't he? I mean, the spirit of a dead person wouldn't be seen ... Mmmm. You being an old friend of his, you'd be one he'd be certain to want to help out, if it was at all possible, wouldn't you, sir?'

Spence smiled, got up and made for the bar. 'I daresay. Let me get you a drink, lass. Then I must be off. What was it now? A dry sherry?'

'Thank you, sir.'

'Anything to eat? Ham sandwich, crisps, curried haddock?'

S I X

It was Thursday morning, 8.30 a.m. on the dot, five days away from the shortest day of the year and as gloomy as a penny candle in an undertaker's water closet.

Frank Spence walked into DI Asquith's office at Castlecombe police station. He sniffed, wrinkled his nose and sighed. The window and door had been closed all day and all night. It was like walking into an exhumation tent. He reached over, opened the window and let in a breath of air. It was cuttingly cold. He turned back to face the room. He could just make out the outline of the desk, chair and cupboard. He yawned, rubbed a hand across his mouth and wondered what he was doing in this stark work box at such an uncivilized time on a cold winter's morning. He had thought he had left clock-watching behind to pursue a comfortable career as a crime writer. That had been the plan, after the force had told him they didn't want him any more. But this return to the grind – be it only temporary – was going to take some getting used to. He sniffed again and looked out through the window at the ominous dark sky with blood-coloured streaks of light showing between black clouds. He reached out for the switch and knocked it down. Ah! That was better. It was surprising what 150 watts could do. Everything always looked better in the light. The sickly institutional yellow and green paintwork conveyed a familiar security to him. He sighed again and unbuttoned his coat. He was about to take it off when the phone rang. He leaned over the desk and reached forward for it.

'Spence.'

'Now then, lad.' It was the superintendent. 'Have you solved the mystery of the sugar spreader yet?'

'No, sir. Not yet.'

'Err,' he grunted sarcastically. 'Well, here's another opportunity for you to flex those famous, overvalued and expensive investigatory muscles.'

'Oh?' Spence said, pulling a sour face.

'A report's just in from a triple nine. One IC male body has been found in a flat over Carrington's bread shop on Thirsk Street. Possible murder. I've sent SOCO, two uniformed and I've left a message for Chester. See if you can clear it up a bit smartish, will you? You've got Gold to assist you.'

'Right, sir.'

The line went dead. He slowly replaced the handset. Things were getting more interesting. A possible murder. His pulse began to pound; that old gentle but insistent throbbing in the chest started again after more than two years in hibernation. The old buzzing sensation in the head returned, that buzz that triggered his extraordinary intellect and prompted him to ask the right questions, sift the replies and uncover the pertinent clues to solve the most perplexing of mysteries. Investigating a case of murder to Frank N. Spence was more than a puzzle, it was a work of art.

There was a knock at the door.

'Come in,' he called.

It was WPC Gold.

'Good morning, sir,' she said brightly.

She was, as usual, immaculately turned out: uniform pressed, hair neat, make-up subtle and adequate.

He looked down at her. She looked almost as nice as a hot bacon sandwich.

'The super's assigned me to you again, sir. Looks like I'm yours permanently.'

He sniffed and shook his head.

'No. I don't think so,' he said dryly as he buttoned up his coat and made for the door.

Her eyebrows shot up and her mouth opened slightly. It turned into a smile.

'Come on,' Spence called back over his shoulder. 'We've got a possible murder. A body's been found.'

Gold's smile vanished. She'd never seen a dead body before. Her hand shook slightly as she reached out to close the door. If she'd had any breakfast that morning, it would have turned over and come back up to say hello.

Do Not Cross blue and white tape fluttered across the front of Carrington's baker's shop, and an unhappy police constable with a pink nose was standing on the step, clapping his gloved hands and stamping his feet. The shop window was in darkness, in contrast to all the other retail establishments in the street, which were all brilliantly illuminated and showing off their Christmas fare.

Busy shoppers, some holding their coat collars round their ears, scurried purposefully along the street, barely noticing the unlit shop, the plastic tape and the shivering policeman. Spence and Gold arrived, got out of the car and bustled up to him.

'Good morning, sir,' the PC said mournfully. Then he recognized Spence, smiled warmly and threw up a salute.

'Oh. I'd heard you were back, sir. Nice to see you. I've read your book.'

'Ta,' Spence said brightly.

The PC and Gold exchanged smiles.

'Where's the body, Tom? And who's with it?'

'In a flat on the first floor, sir. Dr Chester and Ron Dodd are here. And Simon Dickenson.'

The PC turned round, reached out to a knob and pushed open the green door next to the one into the baker's shop.

'There's a door inside leads into the shop, sir. But I don't think it's used. The body is one flight up. There's a floor above that, where an old lady lives ... on her own, I'm given to understand.'

'Right, ta.'

'It's dark in there, sir. There *is* a bulb ... and there's a switch at the bottom but it doesn't light up.'

Spence was about to enter when he turned back to the PC.

'Have this door and these stairs been checked?'

'The door is OK, sir. And Ron Dodd has covered the steps with polythene.'

He nodded, wrinkled his nose and turned to Gold.

'Where's your notebook, lass?'

'Here, sir,' she said brightly, holding it up in her left hand and showing him the pen in the other.

'What you got down? Anything?'

'*Everything*, sir.'

He took the book from her and looked at it. He peered closely at the writing. He screwed up his eyes and shook his head.

'I can't read *that* spidery scrawl,' he said, handing her the book back. 'Didn't they teach you writing at school?'

'I got an A level in English, sir!'

'Looks like a doctor's prescription. You'll have to transcribe it each day. You should've got the time, the address, who is present, and the layout of the door, the baker's shop and the stairs.'

'I've got all that.'

His eyebrows shot up. 'What?'

She nodded and then smiled.

He looked at her and pursed his lips.

'Oh. When we get inside, don't *touch* anything without permission, and don't *walk* anywhere without permission. Write everything down relevant to the enquiry, plus any corresponding replies or information from any witnesses and experts. You understand?'

'I know. We did all that at Hendon, sir.'

'Well, don't miss anything that might be useful later,' he said edgily and turned towards the door.

'Never mind, sir. I've got a good memory.'

Spence stopped and whipped round angrily. 'We don't rely on memory. *I've* got a photographic memory,' he roared. 'But this isn't *The Weakest Link*. Somebody's life might depend on what you remember to write down and what you don't!'

He led the way into the tiny hall, past the internal door to the shop, up to the foot of the polythene-covered stairs.

'Don't touch the handrail,' he snapped without looking back.

Her jaw dropped in horror as she drew back her hand just in time.

They began the climb.

The PC closed the street door behind them, shutting out the light.

The stairway was as dark as a closed up coffin.

Gold breathed in unsteadily and licked her dry lips as she smelled the dust and peered into the darkness. She was very glad to be with Frank Norman Spence.

On the seventh step, there was the sound of something ahead and just enough light to make out the silhouette of a man standing at the top.

'Is that Simon Dickenson?' Spence called.

A light flashed into the inspector's eyes.

'Aye,' a voice said from above. 'Morning, sir. *You* must be on this case, then?'

'Yes, I am,' Spence said, reaching the top and puffing out a foot of breath that came out white. He glanced round and could just see another scruffy staircase on the right, and reasoned that that must be the way up to the top flat.

He screwed up his eyes.

'Can't somebody put a bob in the meter?' he said.

His voice echoed round the uncarpeted stairwell and high ceilings.

'I think the electrics are all out, sir,' Dickenson said, pointing upwards.

Spence sniffed.

'Where's the doc?'

He nodded towards the doorway behind him, where light was filtering through.

'In there, sir,' he said and turned sideways to allow them to pass.

Spence stepped on to the landing and across to the door. Gold closed up behind him.

He peered into the small living room.

He spotted Dr Chester in her conspicuous white overalls bending down over something on the floor near the settee. He glanced round. The room was adequately furnished with a three-piece suite, small table, television set and stool. It had an aluminium sink unit, oven and fitted cupboard against the farthest wall, built in under a window. Everything was basic, old-fashioned, charmless and dusty, but he reckoned he had seen worse.

'Good morning, Doc. You've started without me?'

She didn't look up, but called out, 'Inspector Spence?'

'Aye, with a WPC. Any overalls?'

'No. But could you ask the WPC to wait a while? We're polythened up. I hope you approve, and we're nearly done.'

'Yes. Sure.' He looked at Gold. She had heard clear enough. She nodded and gave a wan smile. She wasn't disappointed. She needed time to come upon dead bodies.

Spence picked his way along a pathway of polythene sheeting the width of a newspaper laid from the door across the wooden floorboards on to a big carpet square to the settee. His shoes made vulgar squelching noises, much to his surprise.

'Is the carpet wet?'

'Sodden.'

'Hmmm. What's happened?'

'A tap was left dripping, and a towel was in the sink. As it got wet, it partly blocked the waste and caused water to flow over the edge of the bowl. It reached the corpse, contaminated its blood and the tainted water eventually seeped into the carpet, through the floorboards and down through the ceiling to the baker's shop below.'

That was unusual. Spence shook his head.

'Hmmm. Nasty.'

Dr Chester looked up. 'It raised the alarm, otherwise the body might have been here a lot longer.'

Spence could now see the doctor was leaning over a dead man laying face down on the floor, with his arms stretched out and palms downwards. The body was partly on linoleum and partly on the carpet. A large area of the carpet around him was stained a browny red colour. He was wearing a T-shirt, jeans, black shoes and red socks. An upturned aluminium foil container with food spattered around it lay four feet away on the carpet.

Spence crouched down next to the doctor and looked at the back of the head of the body.

'Only young?' he said quietly.

'Mmm.' She nodded and with a rubber-gloved hand, touched the back of the head. 'Looks between nineteen and twenty-five or so.'

'Too young,' Spence said gently. He took a moment for quiet reflection. Then he took in a deep breath and said, 'Any ID?'

'No. The landlord knew him, apparently. He's been advised.'

She snipped a few hairs from the nape of his neck and put them in a plastic bag, sealed it and pulled out a pen to mark it.

'Cause of death?'

'Stabbed with a sharp instrument, presumably a knife, into the heart or the aorta. Can't see the weapon anywhere.'

Spence pulled a face then sighed.

'Mmm. The assailant would have blood on him, or her.'

'Hand and wrist at the very minimum, probably the arm and chest as well. Attempted to clean up – hence the tap running and the towel in the sink.'

Spence rubbed his chin. 'Amateur. Somebody who has probably never had so much as a parking fine.'

'Mmmm. Get me the murderer's clothes and I'll get you a guilty verdict.'

Spence suddenly became aware of the unpleasant odour. He eased back but stayed down in the squatting position, looking round.

The doctor noticed and looked across at him. 'He's been dead a few days.'

From that low angle, Spence surveyed the room several times, like a precision camera making panoramic sweeps. He suddenly stopped at a place on the linoleum near the body and zoomed into it.

'What's that?' he said and pointed a shaking finger at a place on the dusty brown linoleum. The buzzing in the head and the vibration in the chest started up. He leaned over to get closer to the place.

Dr Chester turned. 'Can't see anything ... A few drops of water?'

'No. No! You need to be where I am. Something written in the dust.'

She shuffled over, knelt beside him and looked down at the place he had indicated.

'Must be something he "chalked" with his finger just before he died,' he said excitedly.

She stared at the place and then slowly read: 'One ... two ... two.'

Spence nodded. 'Yes, 122. Clear as day. And, considering all the muck round here, I should think it's comparatively fresh.'

She nodded. 'What's it mean?'

Spence pursed his lips. 'Don't know. House number. Car number. It was presumably written by the dead man ... intended to tell us something ... something about the murderer ...'

Suddenly he whipped round and looked towards the door. 'Are you getting all this down, WPC Gold?' he bawled.

'Yes sir,' she shouted energetically. 'Every word.'

'Good. Good.'

He turned back to the doctor. 'We had a PC whose number was 122,' he said, muttering and rubbing his chin.

'Couldn't be anything to do with him. He's dead, anyway. Has the photographer been?'

'Not yet.'

'Will you see that he gets a good shot of that, Doc? So that every half-witted, short-sighted, illiterate member of a dithering jury could make it out. It might be critical.'

'Why don't you stay and see that he does?'

Spence sniffed. 'Mmmm. Maybe I will.'

He pointed to the upturned aluminium foil container of food on the carpet.

'Was the lad disturbed having a takeaway?'

'Looks like it,' the doc replied, 'I'll have to let you know. He may not even have started it.'

He stood up and panned round the room again as painstakingly as he had done from the crouching position. His eagle eye spotted something shiny projecting out from under the settee.

'Have you seen that, Doc?'

She looked where he was pointing. 'Yes. It's a dinner fork. Has his prints on it.'

'Ah,' he said and continued the survey. At length he said, 'How many rooms are there?'

'There's a tiny bedroom and an even tinier bathroom. Ron Todd's in there now.'

The PC put his head round the door jamb.

'Good morning, sir. Talking about me?'

'What's in there? Anything useful? Any sign of anybody else living here? A partner, wife, girlfriend, boyfriend, mother ...'

'No, sir.'

'Nobody else's clothes, gold, money, drugs, porn, weapons, ammunition? You know what'll make my tail wag?'

'There's a wallet on the dressing table ... *and* a mobile phone.'

Spence's face brightened. 'Ah! Have they been dusted?'

'There's prints on the mobile. Nothing I can use on the wallet, sir.'

Spence's face turned to thunder. 'Where's that damned photographer?' he muttered. 'Right, lad,' he called out loud to the constable, 'as soon as the photographer's been, let me have both those items smartish.'

'Right, sir.'

Dr Chester picked up the room thermometer she had placed on the floor by the body, noted the reading, put it back into its case, pushed it into her bag and stood up. 'The body has been here at least two days. I wonder if this room temperature has been constant since he died? That's what I *don't* know.'

'Can't help you there, Doc,' said Spence. 'There's no heating on, is there? No central heating. Mmm. Was the light switched down when you arrived?'

'No. I tried it and switched it back.'

'How did you get in? Was the door locked?'

'No. And it hasn't been forced. Whoever came in was admitted by the victim or had a key.'

'Or it wasn't locked in the first place?'

She nodded.

Spence sniffed. 'What do you reckon about motive, then?'

Her mouth opened a little way. She pursed her lips and said nothing.

'I mean off the top of your head. Robbery, money, drugs, booze, sex, jealous wife, girlfriend? What's your feminine instinct?'

Dr Chester slowly peeled off the plastic gloves, pulled back the white hood, removed the mask and very deliberately said, 'Well, Inspector Spence, I know that murder is your field and that you've built up a not insignificant reputation solving difficult cases in double-quick time. Now I reckon I'm pretty good at what I do too. So I'll make a deal with you. I won't try and outsmart you if you won't try and outsmart me.'

Spence's jaw dropped.

SEVEN

Spence came out of the flat, his mind as busy as a beehive. At the beginning of a murder enquiry it was always so. He followed Gold down the stairs and watched her in silhouette in the meagre light. She wasn't chattering and asking questions in her usual way, but quiet and subdued with her eyes lowered. She kept touching her mouth lightly with her fingertips. She had clearly been unnerved by the proximity of the corpse. It was her first murder scene and Spence thought she had behaved with wholly appropriate reverence.

She reached the bottom and opened the street door. The PC on duty in the stark December wind was still stamping his feet on the shop steps and rubbing his gloved hands. He turned towards them.

'Is there anybody in there, Tom?' Spence said, nodding towards the darkened baker's shop window behind him.

The east wind was still causing the police tape to flutter wildly.

'Mr and Mrs Carrington are in there trying to get s-s-sorted, sir,' the constable stuttered through chattering teeth. 'Are you going in?'

'Aye,' Spence said. 'While we are in there, I should trot across the road to that café. Get yourself a cup of tea and get thawed out.'

His eyes lit up.

'The lass and I will be in here a while, I expect. We'll keep an eye on things.'

'Oh! Right, sir,' he said, his eyes twinkling appreciatively.

The PC raised the tape eighteen inches and opened the shop door for them. A tinny bell danced noisily on a big spring above it.

Spence and Gold dodged down and made their way into the shop.

The smiling PC closed the door behind them.

The baker's shop was only small. It had a glass display counter, with glass-covered display areas along the top of it, and a cash till at one end. The walls were tiled in white and reflected what natural light there was. There were more glass showcases in the two windows.

Incongruously placed in the centre, on top of the counter, was a white plastic bucket.

Spence approached the bucket and peered into it. It was half full of dirty pink water. He wrinkled his nose and looked up at the ceiling; the pink water was accumulating at the bottom of the centre light bulb of a plain wooden five-bulb chandelier. The water formed a globule that dropped into the bucket with an ugly plop every few seconds. The noise was significant and disagreeable. He turned to Gold and pointed upwards.

She looked up, pulled a face and nodded, then scribbled something in the notebook.

It was colder in the shop than it was outside! Their breath came out as white cloud. Spence suddenly realized he couldn't feel his feet. He wriggled his toes. Nothing. He moved around, looking at everything. There was nothing edible on show. Everywhere had been washed down and wiped clean. The showcases and shelves were empty. There weren't enough crumbs to make a crouton. He shook his head and licked his lips.

There was a rustle of clothing. A broad-beamed woman in a white overall, about forty, with blonde frizzy hair, a red plastic cyclamen flower incongruously tucked into it over her left ear and wearing too much make-up appeared at the door behind the counter.

'We're closed, I'm afraid,' she said quickly.

She noticed Gold's uniform.

'Oh,' she said, momentarily disconcerted. 'Police.'

Then she saw Spence. She looked him up and down and switched on a big smile then looked into his eyes and kept looking. She maintained the look as she brushed the front of the overall downwards with her hands, and pushed her big chest towards him.

'I've been expecting you,' she said chirpily. 'We're in rather a mess. Oh! I recognize you. You're that very, very clever policeman, who did … something and had a book published and now they're going to make a film of it. I saw your picture in the paper, *and* I saw you on television. You were very *brave*.'

He smiled, shook his head, then nodded, then shook his head again. 'No. Well, something like that. I'm Frank N. Spence. Acting detective inspector.'

'*That's* the name,' she said, her eyes shining. 'That's it. Frank N. Spence! I remember.' She thrust out a hand. 'I'm *very* pleased to meet you, Mr Spence.'

Her fingers were pleasantly warm and her skin soft; she held his hand firmly – and for longer than necessary. She shook it several times, all the while looking into his eyes and giving him her best Doris Day smile. He reciprocated with much less enthusiasm and was glad to recover it before it was turned into butter. He slipped the massaged limb into his pocket for safety and looked up at the ceiling. Then he nodded towards the bucket on the counter. 'I understand the overflow drew your attention to the upstairs, and to the dead man?'

'Yes, Mr Spence. *That*, and the electric going off.'

She stopped staring at him, turned back to the door in the arch from where she had come and called, 'Russell! It's the police. Come along, dear. You're wanted.'

She turned back again, smiling.

'My husband. He'll be here in a minute. He's just finishing off the oven. We've had a terrible time of it this morning. All our orders have gone to pot. I don't know *what* our customers will be doing for their bread. Some of the pastry lines were ruined. We had some custard tarts spoiled with that … filthy water dripping on them. And we can't do *anything* until that stops running. The lights are fused. The heating's off. There's water all along the electrics. Everywhere is freezing cold. Can't even put the light on. It's a good job the ovens are gas-fired. You got shot at, didn't you? And had to go to hospital. Are you all right now? I must say, you look very strong and fit. Good job you are so young. You can do so much more when you are young, can't you? He won't be a minute.'

She turned back again and called, 'Russell!'

Spence frowned. Then he said, 'You *are* Mrs Carrington? And this is your shop?'

'Yes, of course. Well, no, it's *my* business, but the property is owned by Mr Symington. He's the landlord. But you can never get hold of him. He's always away.'

A very thin man quietly appeared in the archway. He had a long, pasty face and a curly head of fair hair. He was smartly dressed in a white shirt and tie, brown polished leather shoes and a spotless white coat. He had small hands and long slim fingers and he was wiping his hands on a white tea-towel.

She turned towards him.

'Ah! There you are. Come on in, Russell.'

He entered with his back to the wall, taking awkward little sideways steps while looking across at Spence and Gold with the smile of a choirboy. He was clearly ten years or so younger than his wife.

Mrs Carrington reached out to him.

'Come on, Russell, dear,' she said impatiently. She took his hand and pulled him away from the wall into the space behind the counter next to her.

He shuffled up to the counter obediently, and continued smiling angelically at Spence and Gold while wiping his hands on the towel.

'He's not used to strangers, Mr Spence. He's a dab hand at baking, though, and nobody knows that oven better than my husband. Do they, Russell?'

She turned back to him and said, 'This is Mr Spence who wrote that book, Russell. I told you about it. He was on the television.'

'Oh yes,' he said in a pleasant, very quiet voice. 'Pleased to meet you.'

Spence nodded and smiled.

'I was just saying to your wife, it was this leak of water on to the counter that first drew your attention to the body of the man upstairs. Can you tell me exactly what happened?'

Russell Carrington's jaw dropped. He opened his mouth to answer, then looked anxiously at his wife.

'May I answer you, Mr Spence?' she said quickly.

Russell smiled and nodded.

Spence looked from one to the other and then said, 'Yes. Who found him?'

'I did,' she said, turning the corners of her mouth down.

'Tell me about it. Start with first thing this morning.'

She put a hand on her chest and sighed. 'Russell and I got up as usual at four o'clock. We start early in our business, Mr Spence. Fortunately, we live in the back of the shop, so we don't have to travel, especially in this sort of weather. Anyway, Russell got the oven going while I made the breakfast. Well, it's only toast and tea, but we had that and watched the news on television, as usual. Then we got dressed and Russell put the first batch in. He was busy with that while I began filling the showcases. I was bringing freshly baked stock from the cool larder in here. I was just carrying a tray of custard tarts through this door when it happened. The lights went off. The heating went off. Everything went off ... it is *still* off. Even the motors on the fridges died on us. Well, it's happened before, so I put the custard tarts down on the counter, went into the kitchen cupboard and found the candles and a little torch, which I put in my overall pocket. I lit the candles and put them here and there. It was only seven o'clock so I didn't think I could phone anybody ... the electricity people. I brought a candle in here and I began to put the tarts into the display cabinet. The tray felt wet. It was very wet. Then I felt a splash. Of course, it was then that I found out that there was a leak from upstairs. Big drops of ... water were coming from the ceiling rose and down the electric wire on to the counter. Well, I immediately took the custards back. But of course, I had to throw them all away. And I wondered whatever was happening in the flat above ... if he'd left the tap running or the bath was running over ... or what ...'

Spence said, 'Did you know him then, Mrs Carrington?'

'Oh no,' she said quickly, then she said, 'Well, yes, I had *met* him. Came in for breadcakes. Nice young man, he was. Had a lovely tan. I had spoken to him several times.'

Out of the corner of his eye, Spence saw Russell Carrington move slightly. He had straightened up and pulled his shoulders back; his jaw had tightened and the smile had gone. He stared at his wife.

Spence continued: 'Do you know his name? And where he came from? We will need to contact his next of kin urgently.'

'His name was Ronald Kass. He had just returned from the Middle East. He'd been in the Iraqi war. I don't know anything about his next of kin, but I think the landlord, Mr Symington, would know. I think he knew him quite well.'

'Ah. Mr Symington? Where can he be reached?'

'His address is 12 Park Villas, Goathland Road Castlecombe. But he's never in.'

Spence glanced at Gold.

She nodded, smiled and scribbled hard on her pad.

'Thank you. We'll find him. Now where did this man, Kass, work? What did he do?'

'I don't think he'd actually started work,' she replied.

Russell Carrington suddenly jerked into life. 'He didn't do *any* work,' he snapped vehemently. His face was scarlet. 'He was bone idle. He was a ne'er-do-well. A waster. A gypsy.'

Spence and Gold stared across at him, surprised at the outburst.

Mrs Carrington turned and glared at him.

'That's not fair, Russell. We don't know *what* sort of a life he'd had. We don't know *anything* about him. He didn't do *us* any harm. He had just come out of the army. He was unemployed and looking for work.'

Russell Carrington's lips trembled. He clenched his fists and turned away.

His wife's lips tightened momentarily. She turned back to Spence and forced a smile.

'How long had he been living in the flat?' asked Spence.

'About a week,' Mrs Carrington said.

'She used to go up and ... and visit him!' Russell Carrington said, his eyes blazing as red as a baker's oven.

Mrs Carrington's bust rose up like two cottage loaves.

Her mouth opened wide enough to show Spence all her fillings.

'*I did not!*' she bawled.

'Yes, you did!' argued Russell Carrington.

'I didn't.'

'You did.'

'I didn't.'

'You took him some some some ...'

'Oh, *that!*' She turned to Spence, tilted her head slightly, forced a smile and said, 'I once took up some cream buns that were left over, that's all. They would have gone off if we had kept them overnight.'

'And there was that other time,' Russell Carrington said more loudly, spraying saliva across the front of her overall. A vein on his right temple began to throb faster than a Kenwood mixer.

'There *wasn't* another time,' she bawled furiously, her face scarlet with rage. 'Russell. Russell! You are not to get excited like this. It's bad for you. You'll make yourself ill—'

'You took him up that hot stuff from the Chinese,' he shouted, his lips dripping with saliva.

'Only because *you* wouldn't eat it!'

She turned to Spence again, gave him a quick flash of her teeth and said, 'It was a takeaway that *he* wouldn't eat. He said he wanted a poached egg! There's some days, especially Saturdays, when I can't do a full day's work and then cook a meal at the end of it. It's just *too* much!'

'You were up there for more than an hour!' her husband bawled.

'He was asking me if there was a laundry round here. And I was showing him how to work the washing machine, where to put the powder ... and ... Oh really, Russell. You're showing me up. And you are showing *yourself* up. And in front of visitors!'

She turned away from him, sighed, switched on a smile briefly and looked towards Spence and Gold.

'He is a bit upset about everything that's happened this morning,' she said putting a hand to her head. 'Nothing has gone right ... and then finding that poor young man, all crumpled ...'

The door in the archway to the back slammed.

They looked round.

Russell Carrington had gone.

His wife looked after him, bit her lip and turned back to Spence.

'Sorry about that, Mr Spence. He doesn't like it when things don't go his way.'

Spence tried to look unconcerned. 'Let's press on. You said you were the one that found the dead man?'

'Yes. Well, naturally I was worried about the ... water ... I was worried about how much damage it would do. So I unbolted this door – I was still in my slippers – and I went out of the shop into the street and through the street door that leads to the upstairs flats. It wasn't locked. Sometimes it is. I reached Ronnie's flat and knocked on the door several times ... Of course, no reply, then I tried the door handle. It wasn't locked so I opened it and called out ... but there was still no reply. I went in ... I left the door open ... It was ever so quiet. I tried the light switch and *his* lights didn't work either. It was a good job I had the torch with me. It was almost pitch-black. I could make out the silhouette of the windows against the dark sky, but that was all. I could hear the sound of dripping water from the direction of the sink. Then I suddenly realized how cold my feet were. My slippers were soaked ... I was standing in water. I flashed the torch at my feet and then at the sink. Everything was wet through. The sink was full of water and there was a tap running slowly. I turned it off, pulled the towel away from the plug hole and the water ran freely and noisily down the waste. I would have to waken Ronnie. I turned and flashed my torch towards the bedroom door. Then I saw his body on the floor. What a shock! Oh, what a shock. Oh dear. I shall never forget it. Oh. Oh. Oh dear. I *knew* he was dead. I knew he *must* be. He didn't move or breathe or groan or anything. I didn't touch him. I didn't go near him. I shot out of there ... came back here and dialled 999. The rest you know, I think, Mr Spence.'

There was suddenly the loud sound of something crashing and the breaking of glass from beyond the direction of the door in the arch.

Mary Carrington's face changed.

'Russell!' she screamed. She turned and dashed through the door to the back.

Spence and Gold went round behind the counter and followed her.

It led into a small, cosy living room with a gas fire blazing. There was a big cupboard along one wall and a small dining table in front of it. Russell Carrington was standing by the cupboard holding a jar of marmalade and staring open-mouthed in the direction of the fire. Across the front of the tiled fireplace and on the hearth rug a thousand pieces of jagged mirrored glass reflected whatever light there was.

'Oh! What have you done?' Mrs Carrington said quietly, her jaw set, her face scarlet, her eyes blazing. 'What have you broken, Russell? My mother's mirror?'

Russell Carrington pulled his elbows tight into his side, wriggled like a worm and said, 'It wasn't me, Mary. It wasn't me. I didn't touch anything. I was clearing the table. I wasn't anywhere near it. It wasn't me. Honestly. I was just clearing the table. *Somebody* has to do *something*. We both can't stand about *talking* all day.'

She stared at the mess in front of the fireplace.

'What *have* you done?' she said menacingly and walked slowly towards him. 'What have you done to my mother's mirror?'

'It just fell. It just fell. I didn't go anywhere near it. I was over here. I was clearing the table. I was clearing the table,' he babbled frantically. 'Putting the stuff in the cupboard.'

Spence looked up at the ceiling directly above the fireplace. In the poor winter light, it was possible to see the light-coloured wallpaper marked with an uneven dark stain and just below that was a hole as big as a glacé cherry, where the hook in the plaster securing the mirror had been.

'Looks like water has leaked down the wall and weakened the plaster,' Spence said quickly. 'That's caused the hook to come away.'

'Oh,' Mrs Carrington said. She looked up at the wall, across at her husband and then she smiled.

Russell Carrington sighed with relief.

'Oh,' she said gently.

She crossed over to him with her arms outstretched and a smile as broad as a rhubarb pie dish.

They embraced.

Russell Carrington put his arms round the big woman, still holding the jar of marmalade.

They kissed noisily then pulled away from each other and made to hold hands. The jar was in the way.

'What's that you're holding, Russell, my dear?'

'It's only a jar of marmalade, Mary.'

She smiled, took it off him and put it on the table.

Gold's jaw dropped.

'Did you hear that, sir?'

'What?' Spence said gruffly.

'He said, "It's only a jar of *marmalade, Mary*."'

'So what?'

'*Marmalade Mary*!' she said excitedly. 'Wife of your late friend, Wally Walpole. *Marmalade Mary! The curried haddock stall!*'

'So what?'

'He's here, sir. It's a sign. He's helping you. His spirit is with us. He's helping you with this case, like he said he would.'

Spence stared at her, his forehead creased with incredulity.

'*Marmalade Mary*?' he bawled.

'Yes, sir,' she said, her eyes bright and her head nodding earnestly.

'Rubbish,' he growled. 'Let's get out of here.'

EIGHT

They clattered up the uncarpeted staircase of the old building to the second floor, which was also the top floor, and made their way along the short landing that led to the flat. Cheerless light, through a murky window in the high roof above, illuminated the landing and showed up dust-laden cobwebs spun across the corners of the paint-starved walls.

Spence knocked on the door.

'Did you get the tenant's name?' he asked Gold.

'An old lady living on her own, sir. That's all we know.'

He nodded.

There was a long silence.

'Maybe she's hard of hearing.'

He knocked again, louder and longer.

A voice eventually called out: 'Come in. Come in! It's not locked.'

Spence turned the cold brass knob and pushed the door open.

The warmth hit him as soon as he put his nose in the room. A fat woman in bedclothes, a red dressing gown and fur-topped slippers stared at him from an easy chair in front of a powerful gas fire. The warm yellow light shone brightly on to her podgy, lined, scowling face and around the room, casting shadows on the walls and ceiling.

The layout of the room was much the same as the dead man's below but more richly furnished, carpeted and decorated; in addition, there was a bed with a carved wooden headboard pushed up against the wall behind a chaise longue.

The white-haired woman was holding a beaker in one hand and a remote control in the other. A television screen showed a picture of John Wayne on horseback being chased by screaming Apaches across open scrubland; the action was heightened by the enthusiastic efforts of a sixty piece orchestra accompanying the yelling of the Indians. She pressed the remote, the screen went black and the racket died. She looked up over the top of her spectacles at her two visitors and said, 'Yes? What do you want?'

Spence said, 'We're from the police.'

'Oh?' she said. 'Well, come in and shut the door, young man. I'm not so well off that I can afford to heat the entire building.'

'Aye. I'm Acting Detective Inspector Spence, and this is Woman Police Officer Gold.'

'Come in. Come in. Come in,' she said quickly.

Spence closed the door and glanced round the room.

Gold nodded at the old lady, took a sly peep at the fire, smiled and promptly ventured closer to it. She then looked round at the many Monet and Renoir prints and originals of lesser-known artists liberally covering the walls, hanging only two or three inches apart, almost obscuring the lemon and gold wallpaper beneath.

The old lady glanced up at Spence and pointed to an easy chair. 'Sit down here. The young lady can sit on that stool. I've been expecting you. It's about the man downstairs, isn't it? I am not very happy about it, you know. It's not very nice living in the same building as a dead man. Well, what's happened to him? You'd better tell me. I'll have to know, I expect.'

Spence eased himself into the chair next to her and said, 'I hoped you would tell me.'

'I don't know anything about him,' she said stiffly. 'A noisy chap, that's all I know. Very noisy. I have telephoned my son to come from the bank. He'll be able to answer *all* your questions.'

'Does he live here?'

'Goodness me, no. He's married. Lives out at Northallerton. But he sees to *all* my affairs. He works for the bank,' she said proudly. 'You see, I live here on my own … have done for ten years … ever since my husband died.'

'I'm sorry,' Spence said gently. 'And what's your name, might I ask?'

'Mrs Turvey. Rosalind Turvey.'

'Right. Now, Mrs Turvey, what do you know about the dead man?'

'Noisy. That's all I know about him. Terrible racket!'

'What sort of noisy?'

'That pop stuff day in and day out … and very loud. Bang! Bang! All the time. Oh my goodness!'

Gold's head suddenly came up from her notebook. Her mouth was open and her eyes were shining excitedly.

Spence noticed the rapid movement out of the corner of his eye and looked back at her enquiringly.

'What is it?' he said quietly.

She leaned over to him and whispered, 'She said "bang bang".'

'What?'

'She said "bang bang".'

'So what?' he replied tersely.

'That's the place where Wally Walpole lived in Australia!'

Spence's jaw tightened. He wasn't pleased.

Mrs Turvey leaned forward and peered closely at them.

'What's going on?' the old lady asked.

'Nothing,' he said, turning back to her. 'Just a little misunderstanding. You were saying?'

Mrs Turvey glared at him. She wasn't pleased either.

'I don't know ... what *was* I saying?'

'You were telling me about the noise the man below you was making. Was it the radio?'

'Don't know. No. It couldn't have been. It was the same racket repeated over and over again. It would be a gramophone.'

'Aye. And when was this?'

'All the time. It isn't as if it had a tune! It's just noise and drums ...'

'Through the night, you mean?'

'No,' she said, wrinkling up her nose. 'Not *through* the night, but sometimes as late as eleven o'clock. I was going to complain to the landlord. It happened every day. It started at teatime, a week last Monday, and it stopped, finally, after almost a full day's banging, on Monday last at 6.30 teatime, just after the end of the news. That's exactly a week.'

'It stopped on Monday 15th?'

'Oh yes, Inspector,' Mrs Turvey said. 'I'm certain it was *that* Monday night. It was the first night of that new soap, *The Martingales*, all about a family that can't agree about anything. It started at half-past six, straight after the news. I was having my tea and listening to the news and there was that hideous racket banging out on the floor below as usual, and then I was thinking how I would be having to endure another evening of it. And that it would spoil the opening episode. And it's always interesting to follow a new soap series from the very beginning, don't you think? And then, much to my surprise, as the title rolled up on the screen, the noise just stopped ... just like that. And I never heard another peep. Of course, I didn't know that the young man had been murdered. I mean, that's perfectly dreadful. And it frightens me up here all on my own. I told Raymond and he said I mustn't worry. He's a grand lad, you know. I don't know what I'd do without him. And he does look after me. His wife's useless. She never visits. Never see her from one month to the next. She might answer the phone now and again, when I ring, but she wouldn't think of phoning me, or getting in her car and coming here to see if she can do anything for me. The shopping or dusting round or anything. There's a bed made up for Raymond in the spare bedroom *any* time he wants to come and stay, I've told him. He might do, one night. I am so nervous now. He said he would come and stay overnight, if I got too frightened. But I don't want anyone blaming me for coming between him and *her*. Anyway, he meant what he said. He brought a suitcase of spare nightclothes, toothbrush and so on, so that he would be prepared, if I was *really* nervous. He could stop here at short notice. You see, he wouldn't have to go home to her. He could just ring up from my phone and *tell* her!'

'So it was definitely Monday evening, the 15th at 6.30, when the music stopped, and you have not heard it since?'

'Haven't I just said so,' she said, glaring at him. 'My afternoon naps have been impossible. It was wonderful when it stopped. I had a peaceful night that night and I have had ever since. I thought Mr Symington must have let it to him for the week. I thought he had gone, it being so quiet ... It's not much fun being old. Noise is one of those things that gets on your nerves. I know it got on mine. Repetitive, meaningless racket.'

'Did you meet the man? I believe his name was Ronald Kass?'

'No. Never even saw him. I don't get out much, you know. To the hospital once every three months for a check-up. These stairs are difficult. Impossible now. They take me in a chair. That's about all. The policeman said he was found by that funny woman, Mary Carrington. Huh!' She smirked. 'She would be good at finding men.' She sniffed and looked sideways at him. 'Especially if he was a *young* man. Hmmm. She's like her mother before her. That poor half-baked husband of hers ... Anyway, you haven't told me. What did he die of? What happened to him?'

Spence hesitated.

'We're not sure,' he lied. 'The doctor is examining the body. At this stage, we are making preliminary enquiries.'

Mrs Turvey nodded.

Gold's mouth opened as she turned to look at him.

'I suppose he's still there,' said Mrs Turvey. I hope you'll be moving him very soon. Can't do with dead people about the place.' She shuddered. 'It fair gives me the creeps.'

'The doctor will be moving the body away today, Mrs Turvey,' Spence said gently.

The door suddenly opened and a tall, smartly dressed man in a black overcoat entered the room. He closed the door and glanced at Spence and Gold, who returned the look.

The old lady smiled.

'Ah. This is my son, Raymond. He'll be able to tell you anything you want to know. He's very clever. Went to Oxford, got a BA, you know. And has a very senior position at the Northern Bank. They couldn't manage without him. Could they, my dear?' she said, looking up at him with a smile straight out of a saccharine bottle.

Raymond Turvey smiled, firstly down at her and then across at her two visitors. 'You must excuse my mother. She is always saying *that*. It's most embarrassing. I am sure that, if necessary, the bank could *very easily* manage without me. I just hope they don't realize that for the next thirty years or so.'

Spence stood up.

'I'm Acting Inspector Spence and this is WPC Gold.'

Turvey nodded again and smiled. He turned to his mother.

'Everything all right?' he asked. 'I told you the police would be calling to speak to you.'

He looked back at Spence.

'Please sit down.' Then his eyebrows shot up. 'Excuse me, are you Frank N. Spence, the writer?'

'Yes,' he said, trying not to appear pleased that he had been recognized.

The man nodded thoughtfully and appeared to be about to say something.

'Make us some tea, Raymond,' Mrs Turvey interrupted officiously.

'Not for us, thank you,' Spence said quickly.

Gold took his lead and said, 'No, thank you.'

'Well, I need a cup. It's no trouble,' Mrs Turvey said. 'Raymond doesn't mind, do you, Raymond?'

The young man smiled but didn't move.

Spence said, 'No, really. We've nearly finished anyway.'

'My son met the man in the flat downstairs, didn't you, Raymond?'

He nodded. 'Yes. At work. At the bank. I work in the foreign currency department. He came in about a week ago with some paper money from Iraq. Wanted to change the stuff into sterling. But the notes were worthless.'

'Oh? What was he like?'

Turvey said, 'He was in his twenties, pleasant enough ...'

'Do you remember anything else?'

'No.'

'What were these notes? What were they worth?'

'They are worth nothing. He had a 120, I think it was. They were 100 dinar notes, unused, uncirculated. I don't think he was convinced ... about the notes being worthless, I mean. After his visit to the branch, he phoned me several times and said they had come from a very respectable source in Iraq. It was true that they were genuine and had been printed for Saddam, but they had never actually been issued and had been declared valueless by the Bank of England. There were several such caches found, I understand.'

Spence noticed Mrs Turvey pouting and shaking her head impatiently. 'I want a cup of tea,' she said.

Spence said, ignoring the interruption, 'He was new to the town?'

'Yes. Discharged from the army. Nowhere else to go, I believe. He knew Mr Symington, the landlord of this building, though. He was away serving in Iraq too, I think.'

'Oh?' Spence said. He rubbed his chin and looked at Gold. 'It's time we were going, Mr Turvey.'

'Raymond, I want a cup of tea,' Mrs Turvey demanded and banged her stick angrily on the floor.

Spence's car was soon on the high and lonely Yorkshire moors surrounded by grey skies, grass and gorse bushes. He slowed down as he approached a lonely signpost, leaning at a drunken angle. He touched the car indicator stalk and made a right turn.

'Goathland Road, lass,' he declared pensively.

'Yes, sir,' Gold said. She closed the notebook.

The steering wheel whizzed back through Spence's hands as the front wheels straightened up. He worked his way through the gears until he was back in top.

'When you get back in the office, find out if Ronald Kass has any form ... and follow up this sugar business. Widen your enquiries. See if anybody else in the country has been broken into and has had sugar thrown about. You've got forty-three forces nationwide to go at. See what you can dig up.'

'Right, sir.'

He sniffed and added, 'I want this silly little mystery solving. It's daft. It doesn't make sense.'

She looked out of the window at the gorse bushes and heather waving in the cold wind for a few hundred yards then said, 'I heard you talking to the doctor about a number chalked on the floor in the dust, by the dead man, sir – 122, I think it was. I put it in the notes.'

'Aye. What about it?'

'You didn't mention it to the Carringtons or Mrs Turvey.'

'No!' he boomed. His eyes flashed and he glanced back at her. 'And I don't want you blurting it out to anybody either. Keep it absolutely stum. That number is going to put somebody away on a murder charge for a long time,' he said grimly. 'That evidence may only be any use to us for as long as the murderer doesn't know that *we* know about it.'

'Well, how will *that* work, sir? Do *you* know what it stands for?'

'No, not yet,' he said irritably. 'That's another job for *you*, Gold. It'll be a good exercise for you. It'll be a room number, the number of a flat, an account in a bank, a map reference, a key, a locker, a deposit box, a membership number, part of a longer number the man hadn't the strength to finish writing … You'll have to look for places, situations, where numbers play a part.'

Her eyes opened wide and she blew out six inches of breath. 'It could be anything!'

'Exactly. You'll need to concentrate on it. When you go to sleep at night, you need to be thinking about it, and when you waken up in the morning, it should be the first thing you think of – 122. You'll have to be thinking about it morning, noon and night. For the time being, that number will be the justification for you being a policewoman. It is a real test of your detection skills … 122, 122. That number needs to be on your mind, running through your head like the sound of the night train to Dartmoor.'

'But *where* do I look, sir?'

'Wherever there's a suspect, lass! And when you find the link, the rest should be dead simple. We send his clothes to the lab, have the doc go through them, and hopefully, she'll find some contamination. Easy. But you need to be quick. Before the villain has got rid of them … buried them or set fire to them.'

'Hmmm. Well, where do I start? Do you suspect the Carringtons or Mrs Turvey?'

'If *you* suspect them, *you* look there,' he replied earnestly.

'I don't know, sir. I am eager to learn … from you … or …' She broke off, thought for a few moments and then added, 'You know, sir. I am sure your lately deceased friend, Wally Walpole, is helping us.'

Spence pulled a face.

'Yes, sir. I really do,' she added.

'Wally Walpole!' he bawled. Then he wrinkled his nose and said, 'Just because Russell Carrington said "Marmalade Mary", and old Mrs Turvey said "bang bang" it doesn't mean to say that Wally's engineered it. I mean, it would be hard to make a case out of evidence like that, wouldn't it?'

'I don't know yet, sir. At this stage, I don't say it's evidence, just a pointer to you that Mr Walpole is ... around ... or it might mean that he's telling you something *far* more specific.'

'Like what?' Spence replied with a sniff. 'That Carrington murdered the young man? Hit him with a jar of marmalade? Or that old Mrs Turvey shouted at him and frightened him to death?'

'I don't know, sir.'

His hands tightened their grip on the wheel. '*I do.* Somebody stuck a knife into him,' he said grimly. 'That's what killed him. That stuff about Wally is *all* bunkum. He was a good man. A great talker, a good copper, but he's *dead.*'

Gold ran her tongue round her mouth; she said nothing, but thought plenty.

They travelled a minute in silence before they reached a hamlet of twenty houses, a pub and a church. Spence slowed down and looked up at the row of detached Victorian houses, each surrounded by tall, dark coniferous trees and high stone walls. The houses looked across at a long stretch of grey-green moor. In the distance, under the cloudy sky, the dull shades merged and the horizon was lost in mist.

Spence said: 'Now, what number is this man Symington's house?'

'Number twelve, sir,' Gold said closing the notebook and pulling on her woollen gloves.

He nodded.

Fifty yards on, he saw the number applied neatly with white paint directly on to a stone pillar. He hit the indicator stalk and drove through open gates, down the drive, past a big lawn, tall trees and evergreen shrubs to four stone steps leading to the front door. He pulled up and they got out of the car. As they approached the steps, he noted small clouds of smoke emanating from some fire out of sight at the side of the house. He wondered what might be burning; it was a wild and windy day for a garden fire.

They climbed the steps. He pressed the bell and waited.

The door was soon opened by a slim woman, about forty, in jeans and a brightly coloured shirt. She had an orange-brown skin (too much time on a sunbed, Spence thought) wore enormous earrings, he reckoned made from bicycle parts, and was made up with more paint, he guessed, than they use on the Forth Bridge.

He put on his best smile. 'Mrs Symington?'

'Why, yes,' she replied, in a voice that sounded like she gargled in Esso.

'I am Inspector Spence and this is WPC Gold. We are from Castlecombe police. Could we speak to Mr Symington, please?'

'Oh,' she said flashing the aquamarine eyelids. 'I'm sorry. He isn't here. He's in Castlecombe General Hospital.'

'Sorry to hear that,' Spence replied.

'Thank you. He's recovering from an operation. Anything I can do to help?'

'Is he well enough to receive visitors?' Spence asked, ignoring her question.

'I should think so, Inspector. He's in Ward 24.'

'Right, thank you. Sorry to have bothered you.'

She nodded, smiled courteously and closed the door.

Spence turned away, hesitated, turned back and pressed the doorbell button again.

The door opened.

'Yes?' she said. Her eyes opened even wider, pushing her pencilled-in eyebrows almost to her hairline.

'You've a fire burning round the side of the house,' he said, rubbing his chin.

'Yes?' she said, looking at him intensely.

'Erm ... is somebody attending to it? In this wind, I suppose it could soon get out of hand.'

'Yes. Yes. I'm looking after it. I've only just come inside.'

'I'll go round and have a look at it,' he said. He turned swiftly away and made for the steps.

'That's all right,' she said quickly. She slammed the front door behind her and followed Spence and Gold along a path across the front of the big bay windows.

'I can deal with it, Inspector,' she said, running behind them. 'I have dealt with many a fire. It's in a proper incinerator; it's perfectly safe. There's no need to bother. There's nothing burning that shouldn't be. Everything's under control.'

Spence turned the corner, Gold at his elbow. Mrs Symington ran round in front of them, causing her earrings to rattle.

They reached the incinerator. It was the size of the traditional zinc-coated metal dustbin, positioned in a sheltered space between the house and a brick-built garage. They stopped and stared at the black smoke billowing out of the funnel.

'There you are,' Mrs Symington said irritably. 'Perfectly safe. Everything is in order.'

Spence nodded. 'Yes.'

'I said it was all right,' Mrs Symington snapped.

'You did. You did. Better safe than sorry, eh? Right, we'll be off then. I should stay with it ... until it's out.'

He dropped Gold off at the station with more instructions. Then he pointed the car bonnet towards the hospital. He had no problem finding Ward 24. It was the same ward he had been in two years earlier when he had had a bullet removed from his stomach, and it was the same nurse, old flame Maisie Henderson, who was coming down the corridor carrying a file.

As she recognized him, she smiled wryly and gave him an old-fashioned look.

'What's the matter with you then, Shakespeare?' she said perkily. 'What are you doing back here? You look all right to me.'

He shook his head knowingly and looked down at the crisp, starched uniform and the twinkling eyes.

'I am all right, Maisie. It's not for me. I'm looking for somebody. A Mr Symington. His wife said he was on this ward.'

'Not any more, Frank,' she said, shaking her head. 'A right bundle of trouble he was.'

'Where is he then?'

'Don't know. He discharged himself last Sunday. Went out like a blue tornado ... just after his wife visited him.'

'What was he in for?'

'Appendectomy.'

'Serious?'

'No. Routine. But Mr Symington was an idiot. Like all men. Another couple of days, he would have had his stitches out and been properly and safely discharged.'

Spence rubbed his mouth. 'What was he like?'

She smiled. 'What's the matter? Is he wanted for murder or something?'

'I just have to talk to him, that's all.'

She shrugged. 'Nothing special. Not my type. About forty. Suntanned. Just back from Iraq, I think his wife said. Always on the phone. I had to take his mobile off him. Then he used to beetle off down to the public phone.'

'Any idea where he might be?'

She shook her head. 'Try his home. He lives out at—'

'I've just come from there. His wife said he was in here.'

'Oh? Sorry, Frank. Can't help you.'

NINE

Spence parked his car on a yellow line behind the SOCOs van. He nodded in response to the salute from Tom, the constable still on duty, and went through the street door to the flats. A solitary electric lamp was shining above, starkly illuminating the peeling wallpaper and cobwebs. He was glad to see that power had been restored. His footsteps echoed around the high ceiling and alerted DC Simon Dickenson, who had been leaning against the door jamb of Kass's flat. He straightened up as he saw Spence coming up the staircase.

'Afternoon, sir,' Dickenson said, throwing up a salute.

'Aye,' Spence said. 'Is that photographer here yet?'

'Been and gone, sir.'

'Ah. Well, who's in there, then?' he asked, nodding his head towards the open door.

'Ron Todd, sir. That's all. Fingerprint man's gone, body's been collected and Doc Chester left forty minutes ago.'

He nodded and turned into the doorway of the dead man's flat. The light bulb, from a central position in the ceiling, illuminated the room, making it seem quite different. The removal of the body revealed more of the brown/red stain on the floral carpet. The plastic sheeting had gone and he could see that, under better circumstances, the flat could have been a tolerably habitable hole for a person to survive in ... for a short time, anyway.

PC Todd came through the bedroom door dragging an army-issue kit-bag with a long number and the name 'Kass R' printed on it. He also carried a large brown envelope with the word 'evidence' across it, printed in big red letters. He looked up and stopped when he saw Spence.

'Oh. It's you, sir.'

He dropped the bag and crossed over to him.

'There are all his possessions,' he said, nodding at the kit-bag and holding up the envelope.

Spence rubbed his chin.

'Anything I couldn't tell my mother about? Any drugs, money, gold, weapons, ammunition, pornography ...?'

'A hundred and forty quid in the wallet in here,' Todd said waving the envelope.

'No foreign money? Iraqi dinar?' Spence said.

Todd's eyebrows shot up.

'No, sir.'

Spence took the envelope.

'There's his mobile phone in there too, sir,' Todd said. 'And the back of a gold earring: the scroll, I think it's called.'

Spence's face brightened.

'Mmmm. And where was it found?'

'On the floor in the bedroom.'

'Any prints?'

'No. Too small. They're very common. Could have belonged to anybody.'

'Hmmm.'

Spence pulled an earlobe, and then looked back at Todd.

'Any other signs of a feminine presence, lad?'

'No, sir.'

Spence nodded then glanced all round the room. His eyes

alighted upon the cupboard under the sink. 'Anything under there?'

'No sir. Washing-up liquid, soap powder, an old scrubbing brush, a brick.'

Spence frowned. 'A brick? What sort of a brick?'

'Just a house brick. Sort of thing that might have been picked up from a demolition site.'

'Hmmm. Was there a rubbish bin? Dustbin?'

'Yes. There was just a kitchen bin. Not much in it. I have the contents. I'll go through them in the lab. Send you a report.'

'Well, lad, what are your conclusions?' asked Spence. 'What do you think happened? Give us a run-through.'

The constable nodded and slowly crossed over to the doorway.

'Right, sir. Well, I reckon the victim came in, on his own, with a takeaway. And he didn't lock the door. Either he was in too much of a hurry, or the takeaway was burning his fingers, or he was starving and couldn't wait, or whatever. It was a meal with noodles in it, chow-mein, I think. So I expect he got it from the Chinese takeaway, the Golden Dragon, across the road. It's the only one round here.'

Todd reached over to the draining board next to the sink and picked up a piece of cardboard.

'This is the lid. It has silver foil stuck on the inside and it's got some Chinese writing on the outside. Incidentally, the victim's prints were all over it. We've rinsed it and left it here to dry off.'

Spence nodded and held out his hand.

'I'll have it. I'll check it out.'

Todd passed the lid.

Spence glanced at it and slipped it into his inside pocket. He was hopeful that the shop would remember Kass and that

107

it might prove helpful in determining the date and time of death.

'Right, sir. Anyway, he was eating the takeaway with a fork sat on that settee. The intruder came through this door ... It's the only way in. The door, as I said, was not locked. Or the intruder used a key and used it *very* quietly. There's no damage. No signs of interference. There are some smudged fingerprints on the knob but they are probably those of Mrs Carrington from the bread shop below, who I understand found the body and reported the incident via a triple nine. The intruder wore gloves and left no printable fingerprints on the knob, or anywhere else on the scene for that matter. Anyway, sir, I don't think the victim could have heard the intruder—'

'He's not known to be deaf, is he?'

'He was fit enough for the army. I shouldn't think so. I'll check on it.'

'Aye. Do that.'

'Sitting there, he would have his back to the door.'

'Aye. Did he have the telly on?'

'If he did, the intruder must have switched it off.'

'Hmmm. What about the radio? Or records?'

'Discs, sir,' Todd said, correcting him with a smile.

Spence ignored him.

'There's a disc in the CD slot in the ghetto-blaster,' Todd said. 'He might have been listening to that.'

'Well, *play* it,' Spence said irritably. 'He's not likely to be sat here munching on his own in silence, is he?'

Todd pressed the necessary buttons. The red monitor light came on; there was a pause and then a deafening sound blared out from the speakers.

Spence pulled a face and waved his arms angrily.

The racket blared on.

'Switch it off!' he bawled. 'Switch it off!'

The constable grinned and obliged.

'It's The Boggs,' Todd said enthusiastically.

'What's that?'

'A new group. Number one. Top of the pops.'

'I don't care,' Spence growled. 'Never heard of them.'

He wrinkled his nose and pulled an ear. He thought about Mrs Turvey upstairs and wasn't a bit surprised she was upset at the noise.

'Well, I assume he eventually heard or realized that someone was just behind him. He turned, stood up, the take-away fell on the floor at his feet, the fork went flying ... landed over there, under that chair. The intruder shoved the weapon – a blade of some sort, we don't know what sort yet – into his chest cavity. Blood spurted out, sprayed over the intruder, the carpet and the settee, and the victim flopped on to the floor. The intruder would be covered in blood – his face and chest probably, a hand and wrist certainly, trousers even, shoes possibly spotted. He withdrew the knife from the victim, took it to the sink, washed it, and himself, under the tap, wiped himself with a towel, turned off the tap, but didn't turn it off tightly enough ... left it running or dripping. In haste, chucked the towel at the sink, switched off the ghetto-blaster, assuming it had been on, went out, closed the door and disappeared. Meanwhile, the victim summoned the strength to mark out the number, 122 in the dust with his finger on the linoleum.'

'Yes,' Spence said slowly. 'That's about it.'

Todd nodded thoughtfully. 'That number must be closely associated with the assailant and right at the front of the dead man's mind.'

Spence licked his bottom lip with the tip of his tongue. 'Aye. As if it was part of the person's name. Like a police officer's number. Like Spence 122. Or someone in the armed services. Nothing convoluted. On the tip of his tongue, so to speak. His last-ditch attempt to tell us. Mmmm. He'd be in a lot of pain, his head would be swimming, he would be fast losing consciousness. May even have *known* he was dying.'

'Mmmm.'

'Well, go on, lad. Finish it off.'

'Well, when the towel got soaked, it acted as a plug, causing the water to overflow the sink. The doc said he'd been dead two days or more. In that time, the water would have worked its way slowly through the carpet and the floorboards into the electrics ... fused the lights and the power supply in this flat and downstairs.'

'Aye, and then early this morning,' Spence interposed, 'Mrs Carrington said she discovered the lights in her place were out and that water was dripping down into her shop from up here. She said she *knew* the tenant ...' He stopped, shook his head and added, 'How *well*, we may never know. Anyway, she knew the tenant, rushed up here, found the place flooded, the sink overflowing, turned off the tap, saw the body, dialled triple nine ...'

Spence arranged with PC Ron Todd to seal up the flat by fitting a heavy-duty hasp, bar and padlock across the landing door, the only entrance, then he picked up the envelope containing Kass's personal items and made his way back to the police station, to his temporary office.

He had just sat down at his desk when the phone rang.

He reached out for the handset. 'Spence.'

'Aye.'

He recognized the high-pitched nasal voice of Superintendent Marriott. 'I want you, lad. I want you down in my office, smartish.'

There was a click and the phone went dead.

It sounded like trouble. He sniffed, replaced the handset and made his way down the green corridor to the office at the end. He knocked on the door.

'Come in,' the superintendent squawked.

Spence turned the knob.

'Come in, lad. What are you doing? Where have you been?' Marriott snapped, rubbing his nose.

Spence stared at him. He had forgotten just how ugly the superintendent was. He had a nose on him like the spout on a bath tub.

'Shut the door,' he snapped. 'What's the idea of setting Gold on circulating all forty-three forces about these sugar thieves, or whatever they are?'

'What?' Spence said, with a puzzled expression. 'Standard procedure, sir. What else would I do? I'm trying to catch the intruders. If any of the other forces know anything, we would pool the info and—'

'I know *all that*!' he snapped. He stared at him with blood-shot eyes. 'You haven't time to be playing about with *that* business!' he continued. 'You've got a murder on your hands. You can't pick and choose your jobs like that, Spence. This isn't one of your comic-book stories. At the money we're paying *you*, you should be pulling out all the stops to get someone for that murder, not faffing around with a piddling breaking and entering.'

Spence's jaw stiffened. 'But *you* gave me the job of investigating the break-ins ...'

'Aye. But that was before this murder came up!'

'Come in,' Spence called.

It was a smiling WPC Gold, who bounced into the office waving a sheet of A4.

Spence eyed her up and wondered if the cat had managed to get any cream at all.

'I've been looking all over for you,' he lied. 'Where have you been hiding?'

She shook her head as she closed the door. 'I was only in the CID office. I've been *very* busy, sir.'

'Aye,' he growled, 'so have I.' He looked at her closely and said, 'And what have you been telling the super?'

The smile left her.

'Oh,' she said, looking uncomfortable. 'He asked me what I was doing. I told him I was circulating the other forces with the gen about the breaking and entering offences at places where sugar was stored, and asking them to advise if they had any similar experiences on their patches.'

'Oh yes,' he said dryly.

'Yes, sir. And he ordered me to stop immediately. And told me he wanted to see *you* as soon as you came in.'

He pulled a face. 'I've already seen him,' he grunted. 'So what did you *do*?'

'Did what he said, of course.'

Spence wasn't pleased. He wrinkled his nose as if he'd just discovered he'd trodden on something unpleasant in the park.

A smile developed on Gold's face.

'But I had already clicked the send button, sir, and I got an email by return from Manchester, who have had *three* cases in the city and one at Oldham. And they sent a still of the intruder down the wire taken from CCTV they got outside one of the places,' she said confidently. Then, with much aplomb, she placed the A4 sheet with the picture printed on it on the desk in front of him.

Spence eagerly gazed down at it. His jaw dropped.

'Trouble is, sir,' she continued. '*They* can't make anything of it. Nor can I. What do you think? Looks like a dwarf.'

Spence peered at the picture. 'Aye. Not very clear. Night-time. Warehouse yard lights. Hmmm. Is it a dwarf? More like a dog.'

'No. Not a dog, sir. Whatever it is, it only has two feet, not four.'

'Yes. I can just make out two legs with feet at the ends. Could be a chimpanzee, though. A midget? It's like a silhou-ette. Can't see any features. Are they sure this is a photo of the intruder?'

'Their camera takes a picture every two seconds. They checked the tape for the whole night. The night they were broken into, this was the image on it – the *only* image, the clearest image. They say it's *got* to be the intruder. It is dated and timed: 15.12.03. 18:32. That's last Monday, sir. Early evening. Just after they closed.'

Spence looked up, shaking his head.

'Well, we've still got a report to come from forensics on part of a footprint. I hope it's not something with bare feet and hairy! Chase them up but keep it out of the way of the super. All right.'

'Right, sir,' Gold said quickly, then her eyes narrowed as she realized the significance of what he had asked her to do. The consequences of disobeying an order in the force were not to be taken lightly.

'Now we've got to find this chap Symington. He has discharged himself from the hospital and they don't know where he is. I must speak to his wife again. Get her on the phone for me ASAP.'

'Right, sir.'

'And I've got Kass's mobile,' he added, and fished into the brown envelope on his desk and offered it up to her.

She put out her hand then quickly withdrew it and looked across at him. He recognized a flash of trepidation. Her big eyes were bigger than ever and shining like headlights. Her lips moved uncertainly. He knew why she was hesitating. He knew what she was feeling; he'd been there himself, twenty-eight years ago.

'Go on. Take it,' he said gently. 'You've got to get used to dealing with dead people and handling dead people's property. Remember, *they* can't hurt you. It's the *live* ones you've to watch out for!'

He watched her face.

She licked her lower lip, gave him a nervous smile, nodded, then reached out and snatched the phone from his hand.

'I want you to get on to the phone company and get a list of the calls made from it.'

'Right, sir.'

'And I want you to find out if there is any CCTV that covers the street door that leads to the flats. Some of the nearby shops might have overlapping coverage. We could be lucky. But first get me Mrs Symington on the line. I suppose she's in the book.'

Gold nodded and went out of the room, her head buzzing. She hoped she could remember everything.

Spence tipped up the big envelope on to his desk. There was a sealed see-through envelope, which he held up to the light. It contained a gold scroll backing to a stud earring. He pulled out a magnifying glass from the desk drawer. All he could read were the number and letters *9ct*. Then he opened a big brown camel-skin wallet. Inside that was an army driving licence, £140 in notes, and a Part One army pay-book in the name of Ronald Kass. He opened the pay-book. There was a head and shoulders photograph of the young man.

The phone rang.

He reached out for the handset.

'Spence.'

It was Gold.

'Mrs Symington on the line, sir.'

'Aye. Ta.' There was a click.

'Mrs Symington? This is Frank Spence. I've been to the hospital and your husband isn't there. I was told that he had discharged himself on Sunday. Now, it is most urgent that I speak to him.'

'Oh?' she said. 'Really? Discharged himself? Oh dear. Oh dear. I didn't know. Well, I don't know *where* he can be. I know he is very busy. He has a lot on his mind. Oh dear. And he is not well. *He must be mad*! Is it anything I can help you with?'

Spence thought she sounded surprised. He couldn't believe she didn't know her husband had left the hospital. Didn't she visit him or enquire how he was progressing following his operation on a regular basis? The hospital was no more than three miles away from their house.

'Yes,' he fumed. 'You can tell him he is urgently required to report to Castlecombe police station to help the police with their enquiries.'

TEN

The Christmas street lights, providing colour in an otherwise black night sky in the centre of Castlecombe, rattled loudly in the December wind.

Spence stopped the car outside the brightly illuminated Golden Dragon takeaway. It was a small, neat and clean-looking shop with windows each side of a door, located directly opposite the flat where the body of Ronald Kass had been found earlier that day.

As he pulled on the handbrake and switched off the lights, Spence looked up at the door and briefly saw, through the window in it, a small hand deftly turn a swinging sign round from 'Closed' to 'Open'.

He looked at his watch. It was six o'clock. It was time he was at home. He snatched at the car door handle, leapt out of the car, crossed the pavement, up the step and through the shop door. Inside was a brightly lit, white tiled area with four red folding chairs on the far side, and a small counter across the front of an open door that led to the kitchen. High up on the wall above the door and all along the wall was a big neatly painted board that displayed details of the extensive menu. Through the kitchen door, a middle-aged Chinese man dressed in chef's hat and whites bobbed around to the sound of something interesting sizzling and jumping around in hot fat. Blue smoke and the smell of food wafted into the shop.

A young Chinese woman was passing through the opening in the counter leading to the back of the shop. She was young, slim and elegant and wearing a white apron over a dark plain dress; she had pale, smooth skin, long black hair held in a ponytail by a little pink ring, and she wore delicate earrings comprising coral and turquoise bobbles. Her dress came down well below her knees; she had bare legs and skinny ankles.

She closed the counter door and struggled to lower the wooden counter top. She looked up as she heard the shop door close.

Spence smiled across at her.

She looked straight at him but didn't smile back. She turned away and busied herself straightening takeaway boxes and paper bags on the counter top.

Spence looked up at the menu on the wall. The choice seemed endless. There was a long list of dishes, the prices and their numbers. He remembered he was in the business of numbers – one in particular, a three-digit number. He went up to the top and then down. He couldn't see 122 anywhere.

The young woman watched him, picked up a little pad and a pencil, gave an involuntary yawn and waited.

He checked down the list again. He still couldn't see it. Eventually he looked across at her.

'Yes?' she said with her pencil poised.

'I'll have a 122, please?' he said artfully.

She frowned, rattled the pencil between her perfect white teeth and looked back and up at the board.

'There isn't a 122.'

'Oh?' he said, feigning surprise. He rubbed his chin.

'No. Look. At the bottom. The numbers finish at 104

with sweet and sour prawns for four persons.'

'Oh?' he replied thoughtfully, while keeping his eye on her. 'Are you sure?'

'Certain,' she said decisively.

He sniffed. It was hard to hide his disappointment. Then he said, 'No matter.'

Her mouth dropped open. She gawped at him. Then she said, 'Do you want something else?'

'No. Not just now, miss, thank you,' he said with a smile. 'Actually, I'm with the police.'

Her eyes flashed momentarily. She sucked in a mouthful of air and lifted up her head.

'Just making enquiries,' he added.

She put the pencil and pad down on the counter and glanced at the doorway behind.

'I'm Acting Detective Inspector Spence. Might I ask you your name?'

'I'm Primrose Lee. Mrs Primrose Lee.'

The Chinese man in the chef's hat came into the shop from the kitchen. He had apparently been listening.

He glared at Spence. 'What you want?' he said roughly.

She turned swiftly and glared at him angrily.

Spence said, 'Who are you, sir?'

'This is my shop. I am Harold Lee. This is my wife,' he said and he reached out, put his arm round her waist and pulled her towards him.

She reached down to his hand, peeled it off her waist and pulled away. He let her go.

'What you want?'

Spence fished into his inside pocket and produced the cardboard lid found in Ronald Kass's flat.

'Can you tell me if this came from here?' He offered the lid to him.

Lee didn't make any attempt to take it, so Spence placed it on the counter.

Mr and Mrs Lee looked down at it. Then she looked at her husband but he didn't return the look.

'What if it is?' he said robustly. 'We use only best ingredients. We have a licence and we are regularly inspected by town hall.'

'I'm sure everything is satisfactory, Mr Lee. I'm sure the meal was delightful. It's simply a matter of confirming the takeaway came from here.'

Spence reached into his pocket and took out Kass's army pay-book. He opened it to show the photograph of the dead man and held it up in front of them.

When Mrs Lee saw it, she let out a high, piercing squeal, lifted her hands in alarm and dashed off into the kitchen.

Her husband watched her go.

'Wife very upset. Very frightened.'

Spence's jaw dropped. He frowned then quickly said, 'I'm sorry. I won't keep you a minute. I simply want to know if you sold a takeaway to this man and when.'

'Yes. Yes, we did. That's the lid. Chicken chow-mein. Several times,' Lee said irritably.

The miserable squeals of his young wife sobbing could be heard from the kitchen.

Lee pointed at the photograph.

'This is the man who was murdered in the flat opposite, isn't it? We heard on radio news just now.'

Spence nodded.

Lee said, 'He came in about this time ... each ... every teatime for about a week. The last time he came in was Monday, last Monday, because my wife—'

There was another big wail from the kitchen.

Lee broke off.

Spence waited.

Lee turned away. 'I must go to wife.'

'How can you be so sure that this *was* the man?' Spence persisted.

'He was always first customer. Waiting on the doorstep. Particularly notice ... very light blue eyes and tanned face. He was soldier, I believe.'

Spence nodded.

'You are positive that the last time you saw him was this time, last Monday, when he bought a takeaway from you?'

'Yes. Yes. Chicken chow-mein, it was. Yes.'

'Come in,' he bawled.

It was WPC Gold, clutching a paper file.

'Good morning, sir,' she said brightly.

Spence looked up from his desk and frowned.

'What do you want? What have you come in here for? It's only half-past eight. Are you on those multi-vitamins? Don't you like the paintwork in the CID office or something?'

'I thought you'd like to know that Ronald Kass *is* known, sir,' she said confidently.

His eyebrow shot up.

She opened the file and produced a sheet of paper, which she put in front of him.

He wrinkled up his nose as he read down the sheet.

'Hmmm. He *has* been a busy lad. More charges here than a phone bill,' he muttered. 'Hmmm. A con man. Liked the ladies. And stole from them. No, correction: he stole from *anybody*. No, correction: he stole from *everybody*.'

He looked up.

'Where's the list of associates?'

'None known, sir.'

'No associates?' he growled, and rubbed his mouth.

'Worked on his own,' she said.

'Not necessarily.'

He looked up at her and pointed to the chair.

Gold sat down.

He dug into his pocket and produced Kass's pay-book.

'You haven't seen this, have you?' he said. He opened it at the front page and pushed it towards her.

'That was him ... on a good day.'

She studied the photograph of the young man, then nodded approvingly.

'Now there's a real hunk, sir. Those eyes are magic.'

Spence sniffed.

'Last night, I went to the Golden Dragon takeaway. This glamour boy bought a takeaway from there a few minutes after six o'clock on Monday evening. Now it would have taken him a little while to get to his flat, settle down and start eating it – which, I reckon, would take the time close on to 6.30, which was the time Mrs Turvey had said the racket stopped.'

'That's good, sir. Isn't it?' Gold said. 'Pinpointing the time of death.'

Spence sniffed.

'Yes. Suppose so.' He went on. 'Funny thing, though. When I showed this photograph to the young Chinese woman in the shop, wife of the owner, she burst into tears.'

'Did she say anything?'

'No. She ... she just rushed away.'

'To her husband?'

'No. *Away* from her husband.'

Gold looked at him thoughtfully.

He looked back at her.

'Maybe I should to speak to her when he isn't there,' he said wryly.

She looked at the photograph again. 'He'd turn any girl's head, sir. He would have turned mine.'

'You want to be thankful you never met him, lass,' he said earnestly. 'And there's something else. According to Turvey, Kass was repeatedly pestering him about changing some Iraqi currency into sterling. He said that Kass had phoned him about it several times.'

'Probably meant a lot to him, sir. Maybe his only funds?'

'Aye. Probably stolen when he was over there, and smuggled back. Turvey said that he had told him the currency was worthless, several times; but still, it ought to be found. It could have been stolen by the murderer, believing it to have a value.'

'It could have been the motive, sir. It wasn't anywhere in the flat?'

He shook his head.

'Get on to Dr Chester. Get the contents of his pockets: she must have finished with them by now.'

'Right,' she said. 'There's something else, sir.' She opened the file and pulled out another sheet of A4. 'It might have a bearing on this.'

'What?'

'I got a list of his calls from the phone company, sir. There are a few calls ... four, I think ... he made to the Northern Bank ... the last few days.'

Spence's eyebrows shot up. He was impressed.

'That fits with what Turvey said.' He took the list and buried his nose in it. 'Ah! And I see he made a call to the Golden Dragon,' he said excitedly.

'That'd be to the Chinese woman,' she said pointedly.

'Hmmm.' He shrugged. 'Might simply be to order a takeaway.'

Gold smiled knowingly.

'And he made one call to the Carringtons,' he went on, rubbing his chin.

'Do you think that was to ask Mrs Carrington to save him a sliced loaf, sir?' she said sarcastically.

Spence ignored the quip and concentrated on the list. 'There are a few calls to the Symingtons.'

'Yes, sir.'

'They could be to *Mrs* Symington,' he said.

It was Gold's turn to be surprised.

'She's old enough to be his mother.'

'It's a link ... another link to Symington.'

Spence looked up from the list.

Gold stood up to leave.

'A cup of tea wouldn't go amiss.'

'Yes, sir.'

She reached the door.

'Hey,' he called.

She turned back.

'Yes, sir?'

'How you getting on finding that number 122?'

ELEVEN

The phone rang.

He reached out for it.

'Spence,' he snapped efficiently into the mouthpiece.

It was a woman's voice.

'Is that Mr Spence, Frank N. Spence, the man who got shot and wrote that book all about it?'

Spence pulled a face. The facts weren't quite like that.

'Yes,' he replied for the sake of speed and simplicity.

'This is Elspeth Trigger on the switchboard, Mr Spence. I'm new here. I've read your book. I borrowed it from the library. I was going to buy a copy and get you to sign it ... you know ... until I found out how much it was. Will it be coming out in paperback?'

'Erm ... Yes, next year,' he said impatiently.

'Ooooh. You do have a nice voice, Mr Spence.'

'Oh? Is that all you wanted?' he said irritably.

'No. Oh no. No. There's a man wants to speak to you from a phone box ... sounds odd. I don't know if you want to speak to *him*. Says his name is Zack. I don't know what sort of a name that is, but—'

'Yes, I *do* want to speak to him,' Spence cut in. 'Put him through straightaway, please.' If Zack was phoning him at the station, it must be important.

'Oh!' she said, somewhat startled. It was obviously not quite the reply she had expected from him.

There was a loud click and then he heard the familiar Irish voice.

'Is that Mr Frank Spence there, now?'

'Speaking, Zack. What's the matter?'

'Ah! Mr Spence. Gloria has been to see me. Weasel's been on the blower to her. He's very hard pressed for cash. He needs the winnings I'm holding for him. He wants me to meet him and hand it over. He's keeping a very low profile, you understand. He's more frightened than a novice at Newmarket. Then I remembered, *you* wanted to see him, so I thought I'd tip you the wink. Also, if you was willing, you could give me a lift there.'

Spence's grip on the phone tightened. The possibility of gleaning any information on the jewelled Salamander and the men with murderous intentions was too good to miss.

'Certainly, Zack. Where and when?'

'Soon as you loike. It's about two laps out of Castlecombe.'

'Where are you now?'

'In a phone box outside the Fat Duck.'

'Stay there, Zack. I'll be with you in five minutes.'

He slammed down the phone and four minutes later stopped the car outside two adjacent phone boxes on the small cobbled area between the Fat Duck and the Northern Bank in the centre of town. He saw a figure in a raincoat and a hat pulled down to shelter him from the wind, holding a white stick.

Spence jumped out of the car.

Zack stepped forward from behind the telephone boxes.

'Hello there, Mr Spence,' he said. 'I'd recognize your step anywheres.'

'I'll put you in the back, Zack. It'll be safer,' he said as he swiftly opened the door and assisted him into the rear seat.

'Thank you. Thank you. It smells like a new car, Mr Spence. Does it belong to you or is it a police vehicle? I don't travel well in police vehicles.'

'About a third of it belongs to me,' he replied while fastening his seatbelt. 'The rest is owned by the Mercantile Credit Guarantee Company of Basingstoke.'

The Irishman smiled.

'I shouldn't have asked. You have overwhelmed me with a surfeit of information. I'm a nosey old divil, I know.'

'That's all right. Now, where are we going to?' he said, letting in the clutch and releasing the handbrake.

'Ah. Do you know Rabbitspaw Bridge at the bottom of Hare Lane, the back road to Whitby?'

'Aye. Know it well,' Spence said.

'I was to go down the left-hand path leading to the south side of the stream and wait underneath the bridge.'

'Right,' he said and put his foot down determinedly on the accelerator.

'I've been thinking. I hope the water doesn't smell any, Mr Spence. With my chest, I'm quite allergic to bad odours.'

'It won't smell, Zack. It isn't stagnant. It's a slow-flowing stream. Well, it *was*. Very pleasant, it used to be – a bit of a beauty spot. I used to walk Mrs Spence round there before we were married, a hundred years ago.'

Zack shook his head. 'Ah. A lot of water passes under a bridge in a hundred years, Mr Spence,' he said with a grin.

'It was very beautiful. I remember seeing fish there in clear water.'

'I've been over that bridge many a time when going to Scarborough Races, but I nivir stopped to go down by the actual water's side. I'm not really a man for … for water.'

'No. No,' Spence said.

They both smiled.

Two minutes later they arrived at the bottom of Hare Lane. There was a small parking area for two cars on the right. Spence drove into it, pulled on the brake and switched off the engine.

He got Zack out of the car and locked it up.

'To get on to the south side, we'll need to go down the nearest path,' Spence said. 'Put your hand on my shoulder, there.'

'Thank you, Mr Spence.'

They set off down the path under the bare trees, kicking their way through fallen leaves and stepping noisily on brittle twigs. It was only twenty yards.

'Have you got the money?' asked Spence.

'Aye. Sixty pund.'

They arrived under the bridge. The path was about four feet wide. Spence positioned Zack back against the wall.

'Stay there, and you'll be safe,' he told the blind man.

'Thank you,' he said.

Their voices reverberated deeply and loudly under the low arched bridge.

Zack ran his hand over the damp stones to confirm his bearings. He was in no mind to experience the sensation of taking a careless step and finding himself up to his waist in near-freezing water. He stood there, quiet and motionless, listening.

Spence peered over the edge of the path and peered down into the water. He thought he could see a shiny pink fish dodge around some pretty water plant. He looked across at the path at the other side of the stream. That was even narrower, perhaps only two feet wide.

The Weasel was nowhere to be seen or heard.

Spence rubbed his chin. 'Do you think the Weasel will show up, Zack, with me here? I am not exactly one of his favourite people.'

'He'd rather meet up wid you than wid the villains that chased him out of Castlecombe House Hotel that night, I can tell you,' he replied with a grin.

Zack suddenly held up his hand. He listened a moment and then said, 'He's not far away, Mr Spence. I know it. I can hear him.'

Spence could only hear the slightest gurgle of water from the movement of the stream. He looked to his left and right and then he suddenly saw the branches of a wild cupressus, near the bridge support at the other side of the water, shake. A figure jumped out of it and landed solidly on the tow-path with the mere clatter of boot studs on stone.

It was the Weasel in his smart suit, with his long nose and whiskery face.

'I'm here, Zack,' he said and stared aggressively at Spence. 'And what did you have to bring *him* for? A copper, I ask you!'

'Ah! *There* you are,' Zack said, much relieved. 'I've got your money. And Mr Spence isn't a proper copper any more, you know. They've put him out to pasture since he stopped a bullet.'

'I heard. And he wrote a book. And made a million. And they say crime don't pay. Huh!' he said sneeringly.

Spence peered across the stream at the little man.

'*Listen to me*, Weasel,' he began. 'Four days ago, a man was murdered. He was a petty thief, not unlike you. A man who charmed the ladies, took their money, lied to them, stole from them – and anybody else he could deceive.'

Spence spoke icily and deliberately.

The little man stared back at him, his nose quivering like a mouse just getting a whiff of the cheese.

'Here. I don't take money from women!'

'He wasn't much of a man,' Spence continued, 'but he didn't deserve to be murdered. And it was a nasty, cold-blooded killing with a sharp instrument. Furthermore, the man was on his own, in his own home, eating his tea, listening to his gramophone, minding his own business. It could have been *anybody*. It could have been *you*.'

Weasel's right eye twitched.

Spence saw it. He continued.

'Now, I know you're a crooked little man – you can't even *think* straight, never mind *go* straight – and you're likely to remain so as long as you live, but you might *know* something … something that could help me put this murderer away. The murderer that has *you* at the top of his list.'

Weasel's right eye twitched again.

Spence maintained the pressure.

'You don't want to help a murderer, do you? Not when you might have some information that might help put him away.'

'What you been telling him, Zack?' he squawked.

Spence hung on to the initiative.

'Now, I'm not interested in your petty little schemes. Even if I could afford the time to catch you, get the evidence, and charge you – which at the moment, I can't. In any case, it still wouldn't take the murderer off the streets, would it? As long as he is free, he could come for *you* any time he chose.'

Weasel's arm and the back of his hand began to shake.

'Here! Don't pick on me, Mr Spence,' he said, his eyes flashing like the chief constable's buttons on Remembrance Sunday.

'If you know anything, Weasel, *tell him*,' pleaded Zack. 'It can't do *you* any harm, and it *could* save your life.'

Weasel licked his lips anxiously.

'Aye, well. Erm ... it depends ... I mean ... what do you want to know?'

'Three men chased you out of Castlecombe House Hotel,' Spence said quickly.

'Yeah. Well, I wasn't doing any harm. I was only in there having a drink, I mean,' he lied.

'Never mind that,' said Spence. 'Describe them. Take the one who made the threat first ... the one who said he would split somebody's gizzard.'

'Yes, well, I didn't get a close look at him, but he was ugly. I mean really ugly. He was tallish, smartly dressed in a dark suit, brown hair, I think ...'

'Anything else? Did he wear glasses? Speak with an accent? Did he wear a raincoat or overcoat? Collar and tie? How old was he? Was he carrying anything? A case? A stick? Anything? Was· he smoking? Any mannerisms? Peculiarities?'

'He didn't wear glasses. No accent. Yes, he had a collar and tie. I don't think he was carrying anything. He was in his thirties or forties, I think. I don't know about anything else. I didn't see him close up, you know. It happened so quickly. And I was after getting out of his way, not clocking him in.'

'And the other chap with him in the room ...'

'Him? He was much younger. Wore jeans and something on top ... can't remember what. A coat of some sort, I think.'

Spence rubbed his chin. He couldn't conceal his disappointment.

'Anything else?'

'No.'

'You saw their feet from under the bed, didn't you?'

'Yes. There's a thing,' Weasel said, brightening up. 'Yes. They were both wearing black shoes, clean and polished.'

131

Spence wrinkled up his nose and sighed.

'Black shoes. Clean and polished.' He ran his hand through his hair impatiently.

'Yes. And one of them was wearing red socks. The young one.'

Spence rubbed his chin. There was something. 'Red socks?' Kass was wearing red socks. Could be a coincidence.

'Aye. I remember that.'

'Hmmm. What about the third man?'

'He was an old geezer. I didn't see much of him. He was ugly an' all. Short, squat. Smart suit, collar and tie.'

'Did he have a moustache, wear specs? Did he wear a hat, overcoat, gloves? Did he carry anything? Did *he* have any mannerisms or peculiarities?'

'No.'

'Are you sure?'

''Course I'm sure.'

Spence shook his head. 'I hope you are never a prosecution witness in any case I *may* bring to court,' Spence snapped, and whipped round to the Irishman.

'Give him his money, Zack, and let's get out of here.'

'Come in,' he bawled.

The door opened. It was Gold. She was carrying a polythene bag with the word 'Evidence' printed across it in red.

'You're back, sir. Any luck?' she asked eagerly.

Spence looked across at her. 'Where've you been?' he growled. 'Squeezing your spots?'

She shook her head and smiled. 'I've just got back from the lab, sir. You wanted the contents of Kass's pockets.'

He nodded and mimed for her to tip the bag out.

'What's the matter?' she said.

He looked up at her and grunted, 'Weasel hardly knows

his own name. Walks about with his eyes shut. All he knows is that he saw three men, one old, one young and one in the middle. Like the three bears.'

'That all, sir?'

'The young one was wearing red socks.'

'Kass was wearing red socks.'

'Yes.'

His eyes brightened as the items rattled on the desk.

Gold produced a sheet of paper tacked on to the bag and read from it: 'One key. Two pounds and twenty-four pence sterling. One Swiss-army-type penknife.'

Spence's jaw dropped.

'That all? No Iraqi money?'

'That's all that's down here, sir.'

He shook his head.

'What's happened to that money? What has happened to that Iraqi currency? Turvey said there were about 120, 100 Dinar notes.'

'That's a motive, sir.'

He shook his head. 'Not worth a light.'

He reached out for the bulky penknife. He opened the blades, and all the additional tools. The blades looked dangerously sharp, and the corkscrew and all the other ancillary implements were heavily worn.

'Looks like he's been demolishing a castle or burrowing his way out of a prison cell or something … and recently.'

He pulled out all the blades and tools in the knife, put it on the desk and stared at it. After a few moments he stood up, went over to the office window and stared out. He rubbed his chin, turned to Gold and said, 'Well, what do you think, lass?'

'It's quite a weapon, sir. You could do a lot of damage with a thing like that.'

'Aye. But why are all the tools so badly worn? I've seen blades over 200 years old in better nick.'

He returned to the swivel chair and dropped into it.

She shook her head.

He reached across the desk for the key. He turned it over. It was just an ordinary two-lever key.

'Does this fit the door to Kass's flat?'

She looked up from the notes.

'It doesn't say.'

His jaw stiffened.

'I'll soon find out,' he said, his eyes flashing. He pushed the key in his pocket and leapt to his feet. 'Get me Simon Dickenson on the line, quick. I'm going out. And while I'm gone, there's something important I want *you* to do.'

He opened the middle drawer of the desk, took out Kass's army pay-book and handed it to her.

'Here. Ring up army records. Find out if Kass was hard of hearing or not. And while you're on, find out about his conduct and what he actually *did* in Iraq.'

Spence reached out for his raincoat.

Gold's mouth opened. She picked up the pay-book.

Spence stabbed an arm into the coat sleeve.

'Well, come on, lass. Chop chop. Get me Dickenson on the phone now!'

TWELVE

DC Simon Dickenson unlocked the heavy padlock, lifted it out of the hasp and stood back from the door of Ronald Kass's flat.

Spence turned the knob, pushed open the door and wrinkled his nose at the smell of fusty carpets and damp plaster drying out from the recent flood.

He gazed inside. It was as quiet as an undertaker's cat.

The eerie, dusty little room was meanly illuminated through the dirty window over the sink. He reached out and switched on the light: the 100 watts through the dusty yellow shade merely changed a dismal black-and-white scene to an equally dismal one in sepia.

'If you give me the key, sir,' Dickenson said, 'I'll see if it fits the lock.'

Spence turned back, fumbled around in his pocket, found the key and handed it to him.

Dickenson shoved it in the lock, turned it, turned it back, withdrew it and handed it back to him with a nod.

Spence couldn't stop himself gazing across at the settee and the blood-stained carpet in front of it and recalling Dr Chester leaning over the crumpled bundle of red-stained clothes. He broke away and went over to the sink under the window, bent down and opened the cupboard beneath it. He reached in and found the item that had been at the back of his mind since Dickenson had told him it was there. It was the house brick. He picked it up and placed it on the draining board. It had several bits of grey cement still firmly bonded to it, and had clearly been made more than a hundred years ago.

Dickenson came up to him, glanced at the brick and said, 'Behind the pictures, I suppose, would be the best bet, sir?'

'Aye,' Spence said, looking round the room. 'There's only the one in here.' He pointed to a cheap frame of a print of a black girl holding a vase; it was hanging on the wall where a fireplace had originally been built.

Dickenson lifted the picture and looked behind it. There was no joy, only more yellow wallpaper. He lowered it. The two men then crossed to the bedroom. There were no pictures at all on the walls there, only a small bathroom cabinet with a mirror that constituted the door; it was fitted over a washbasin opposite the foot of the bed. A door led out of the bedroom. Spence went through it into the tiny bathroom, which had an unpretentious shower cubicle squashed against a WC. He looked round the room. The walls and ceiling were covered in white waterproof paper, the floor with white lino tiles. There were no pictures or mirrors fixed to the walls. He sighed as he turned back into the bedroom. Dickenson was by the door; their eyes met. He shook his head and pointed at the little bathroom cabinet.

The constable went up to it and pulled open the door. Inside was a tumbler on a glass shelf. He removed the tumbler, slid the shelf out and put both glass items carefully in the bottom of the sink. He then felt carefully around the back of the cabinet. It seemed solid enough and did not appear to have been disturbed.

Spence stood back against the foot of the bed, watching.

Dickenson eventually gave up the examination of the cabinet, replaced the shelf and the tumbler, closed the door and looked round at him.

Spence sniffed, came up to the sink. He put his hands underneath the cabinet and lifted the whole thing up an inch, which freed it; he then eased it back over the heads of securing screws in the wall to reveal a crude hole, with printed paper hanging out. His pulse increased as he identified Arabian script, the figure 100 and head and shoulder representations of Saddam Hussein in dark brown ink on crisp, cream-tinted paper. He quickly lowered the cabinet on its back on the bed and looked knowingly at Simon Dickenson. The PC smiled, dug into his pocket and produced two envelopes containing plastic gloves. In silence, they ripped open the wrapping and eagerly snapped the gloves on to their hands. Spence gathered up the notes and fed them into an evidence bag held open by Dickenson over the sink. Spence didn't count the notes but he reckoned there would be 120 100-dinar, notes which was the number Turvey had said Kass had wanted to exchange for sterling. When they had removed all the notes, he spotted something small and glinting in the back of the cavity among cement dust. He reached in for it with a finger. It wasn't easy to pick up in plastic gloves. It was a small piece of gold jewellery with turquoise stones and a half seed-pearl set into it, about an inch long. It had a projected end to insert into a pierced ear. The scroll that had already been found probably fitted it. He thought it was a pretty little piece and very interesting. He dropped it carefully into the bag, sealed it and wrote 'Found behind bathroom cupboard in bedroom, 19th December 2003'.

He thrust it into his pocket and then looked round the room while rubbing his chin. Kass must have deliberately hidden the piece of jewellery there. Did a lady friend drop it or lose it and he had found it later? Was he hanging on to it as a sort of keepsake? If it could only talk, what tales it might be able to tell.

'I got through to the adjutant's office eventually, sir,' Gold said. 'The clerk looked up his records. There was nothing wrong with Kass's hearing. He was in excellent health when he was discharged ten days ago at the rank of private. He was in the Army Catering Corps, where he served most recently in Iraq as catering stores clerk. His conduct was excellent.'

'You spoke to his CO?'

'Couldn't, sir. His CO is on leave.'

Spence pulled a face.

'But I got his *name*,' she said, with a meaningful stare.

'Yes?' he said glumly. 'So what?'

She smiled knowingly.

'Well,' Spence growled, 'are you going to *tell* me or do I have to fetch back a stick and beg?'

'It was Symington, sir. He's a captain in the Army Catering Corps. And his address at Park Villas, Goathland Road, Castlecombe, confirms it's the same man.'

Spence's mouth tightened. 'We really *do* have to see that man. He has history with Kass. He owns the flat he lived in.'

The phone rang. He reached out for it.

'Spence,' he snapped into the mouthpiece.

It was the talkative receptionist. 'I have a young lady in reception wants to see you, privately, she *says*.'

'Yes, what's her name?'

'Mrs Lee, she *says*.'

Spence blinked.

'Right. Please ask her to wait a minute.'

He slowly replaced the phone, and thoughtfully massaged

the lobe of his ear between finger and thumb. 'There's a thing,' he muttered. 'The tearful little lady has something to say.'

Gold looked up.

'What's that, sir?'

'There's a little Chinese lady in reception, lass ... Mrs Lee ... Show her in here and then leave us for five minutes.'

Gold went out and returned a few minutes later. She ushered Mrs Lee into the office and left.

The young woman looked very serious. She wore a plain black dress and pretty garnet and pearl dangly earrings.

'Please sit down. Now, what can I do for you?' Spence said, smiling down at her.

Mrs Lee took the chair and said, 'I wanted to explain about yesterday, Inspector Spence. I was so upset at seeing a photograph of that man ... a stranger, well, he *was* a stranger. I ... we were just getting to know him ... Being murdered like that and him not long here in the town ...'

Spence frowned. He wondered where she was going. 'Yes?' he said encouragingly.

'I didn't want you to get the wrong impression. My husband thought that you *might* be thinking that ... well, that I may have known him better than ... more than ... maybe ... because of me breaking down like that. It was, perhaps ...'

Spence could read between the lines; he'd been doing it for twenty years.

'You got to know him pretty well, didn't you? In a very short time,' he said bluntly. 'And your husband had no idea – not until the news broke yesterday.'

She realized what he was implying. 'No! It was *not* like that.'

'Ronnie Kass phoned you from his mobile.'

She hesitated.

'That was to order a takeaway, that's all.'

'He only lived across the way. You made a delivery?'

'Just the once.'

'With a man like Kass, *once* is enough.'

Her fists clenched tightly. Her eyes shone like cats' eyes.

'It's not how it looks, Inspector,' she said, an octave higher.

'You were seen, Mrs Lee,' he said dryly. Spence always could lie convincingly if he thought it was morally justified.

Her jaw dropped. The pretty earrings shook.

'Who by? No. If my husband thought that—'

'What do you know about Ronald Kass's murder, Mrs Lee?' he said quietly, staring into her big brown eyes.

'Nothing.'

'How much did your husband hate him?'

She sucked in a lungful of centrally heated police-station air and shook her head.

'I don't … I don't know what you mean,' she said majestically. Spence thought it was her turn to lie.

'Did you lose an earring?'

'What? Yes. No. Yes. In the kitchen …'

'In the bedroom,' he replied heavily.

She stood up, her face the colour of a traffic light stuck on stop.

'You don't believe anything I say.'

'You don't say anything I believe.'

'I came to say that my husband and I had nothing to do with Ronald Kass's death.'

'All right. Thank you, Mrs Lee. You've said it.'

'I hope you believe me.' She made for the door and then turned back. 'Perhaps you'll let me have my earring back?'

'Of course. It's an exhibit at the moment. You can have it

when I've got someone safely and properly banged up for Kass's murder.'

Mrs Lee didn't reply. She turned away, put her hand on the knob and pulled the door towards her as WPC Gold, on the other side, was about to knock.

'Are you leaving?'

She didn't reply. She looked back at him, her mouth open, her eyes shining.

He took it as a 'yes'.

'Thank you, Mrs Lee.' Spence turned to Gold. 'Take Mrs Lee to reception please,' he bawled.

The door closed.

The phone rang.

'What now?' Spence said, but there was nobody in the room to hear. He reached out and snatched up the handset. 'Spence!'

It was the civilian telephone receptionist again.

'There's a strange young man to speak to you, Inspector. He seems in a bit of a state. Says his name is Russell Carrington.'

Spence silently groaned. He really wasn't in the mood for that peculiar man.

'Right. Put him through.'

There was a click and then a small, excited, high-pitched breathy voice said, 'Hello. Hello. Is that Inspector Spence?'

'Yes, Mr Carrington,' he replied evenly. 'I'm here.'

'Ah! It's my wife. She's missing,' he began excitedly, his voice reaching top C. 'I'm very worried.'

Spence made for his car and drove over the limit through the streets of Castlecombe, arriving outside Carrington's bakers shop on Thirsk Street in record time. He parked on the yellow line and leapt out of the car. He charged into the shop, making the bell jump wildly round its spring. He looked round but there was nobody to be seen. He looked at the closed door in the arch behind the counter and began to cross purposefully towards it.

Then, from below the showcase mounted on the counter crammed with loaves, a curly fair head and white face with small piercing eyes rose up. It was Russell Carrington. He looked immaculate in his smart white coat. He had an untidy dab of flour at his temple. His head was shaking uncertainly; the corners of his mouth were turned down.

'Has your wife turned up? Have you heard anything?' Spence said urgently.

'No,' he replied and shuffled sideways until he was fully visible behind the serving counter. He ventured a small embarrassed smile and began agitatedly to wipe his hands on a tea-towel he was holding.

'No. I don't know where she is. I've no idea where she is. And I don't know all the prices. I don't know how much she charges for the custards.'

'Where did she go?' he said.

'I don't know. I really don't. The last I knew, she was in here with an old woman, a customer. I went out back to get some more large whites ... It's Friday. Everybody wants bread for the weekend, you know. I heard the shop bell – that would be the customer going out. But when I got back, the customer had gone and *she* had gone as well. She must have gone out through the street door. She didn't come this way. And it's so cold. She never does that. She never leaves the till unlocked, but she did. She always told me, if you leave it unattended you must lock it up.'

'How long has she been missing?'

'Oh, about an hour now,' he said. 'Customers keep coming in and wanting things and I don't know what to charge them. I have to make it up. She does all the serving, you see.'

'Who was the customer she was with? Would she have gone out with her for some reason?

'No. I don't know.'

'You've no idea where she's gone to?'

'I told you. She's missing. I don't know where she is. She'll have gone with a man somewhere. She doesn't need an excuse any more, Inspector. She doesn't bother to cover it up. She's blatant. No. Any opportunity and she's off. It's going to be a *terrible* Christmas,' he wailed.

'Where to? *Where* would she go to?'

He shrugged.

The shop door suddenly opened, causing the bell to ring. Spence turned to see the sturdy frame of Mrs Carrington in a white coat, full war paint, flower in her hair, looking hale and hearty in the doorway. When she saw Spence, she blinked and twisted up her tomato-coloured lips to form a smile.

'Hello, Inspector,' she said brightly, and closed the door.

Spence looked at her with eyebrows raised.

She sensed something was wrong; her mouth dropped open.

'What *are* you doing here? Is anything wrong?' she asked in surprise.

The door behind the counter also closed: Russell Carrington had made a hasty retreat.

'Oh, Inspector,' she said with a concerned look. 'Whatever has brought you here?' Then she forced a smile, waved a finger and, in a voice she might have used with a four-year-old, said, 'Oh, I can see you'll be putting me in one of your books yet.'

Spence wasn't pleased.

'I had a phone call from your husband,' he said evenly. 'He was worried about you. He said you had disappeared.'

Her mouth dropped open; her face went scarlet; her lips tightened. '*Ho!*' she hissed. '*Ho!* I bet he's been telling you the most outrageous stories about me, Inspector.' She clenched her fists angrily and shook them, causing her bosom to shake. Then she stormed angrily round the shop to take up position behind the counter.

'No,' he lied and shook his head. Unusually, he didn't quite know what to say. 'Now that you're back and if everything is ... all right, I'll—'

'*I know he has,*' she said in a voice of thunder. 'Well, I'll *tell* you exactly where I've been.' She began to straighten the wrapping paper on the counter in front of her as she spoke. 'And I bet Russell has seen me going through that door and knows very well. I've been standing at the bottom of the stairs of the flats, not six yards away from this very spot, listening to the troubles of that dear man, Raymond Turvey. How his mother has such pain in her feet and legs with arthritis. And how he turns out twice a day, every day, to check up on her and make sure she's as comfortable as possible. How devoted he is to her. How he and his wife haven't been away on holiday for three years because she's not fit to be left. That's where I've been. That man, Raymond Turvey, is a saint. And his wife has trouble with her nerves too. They've been married eight years and still no children. It's a shame, it really is. And he's such a nice, healthy, strong young man. And he's got beautiful teeth ... and a lovely smile. And his hands ... His hands are ... He's got a good job at the bank – head of his own department. I have no idea what Russell has been telling you but I do hope you'll take it all with a grain of salt, Inspector.' She sniffed. There was a small tear in her eye. She put her hand to her face. 'I don't know what I am going to do with him.' She sniffed again.

Spence stood there, expressionless. He was considering how he might make an early exit without being unkind.

'Oh dear. I'm sorry, Inspector,' she said, and reached into her overall pocket and pulled out a tissue. As she withdrew her hand, a small ball of red wool dropped out and rolled on to the floor somewhere behind the counter.

Spence saw it and pointed down at the floor.

'You've dropped something.'

'Have I?' Her mouth opened. Her eyes flashed. She bobbed down quickly, grabbed it and stuffed it back in her pocket.

'Just some … old darning wool,' she mumbled and turned away.

Spence thought a moment. He was certain that she hadn't wanted him to see that ball of wool.

Spence spotted the white-painted number twelve on the stone pillar and turned left up the drive. He parked the car at the front of the house, walked up the four stone steps and pressed the bell. The door was answered by the tanned and colourfully dressed Mrs Symington.

'Oh, it's you,' she said, and smiled ruefully. 'Good afternoon. So soon. You were here yesterday. The policeman who is a great detective, writes novels and is a part-time fire warden. On your own today?'

'Good afternoon. Yes. I still need to speak to your husband, Mrs Symington.'

The woman leaned against the door jamb and folded her brown arms. 'I'm sorry, Inspector. He's still not in.'

'If I do not make contact with him soon, Mrs Symington, I shall assume that he is deliberately avoiding me. He is urgently required to assist us with our enquiries.'

'I am sorry, Inspector, but he *isn't* in. He hasn't been in for a few days.'

'Well, where is he?'

'Out and about ... I don't know. He's on leave. Catching up with old friends, I suppose,' she said unconvincingly.

Spence wrinkled his nose. 'Your husband is a significant witness in a murder enquiry. Since seeing you yesterday, I discover that he was the victim's, Ronald Kass's, commanding officer, as well as owning the flat where he was found murdered.'

'Yes. I heard about that. You're investigating Ronnie Kass's murder?'

'Yes.'

'How dreadful,' she said, looking momentarily sobered by the news of a death, then she lightened up. 'I met him. What a handsome young man he was. Wasted in the army, I thought. Could have made a big career in the theatre or in films, don't you think?' She gave him one of her big smiles, showing off her small, even teeth and bright eyes, which contrasted with her tanned skin.

'Where did you meet him?'

'Here, in this house. He accompanied my husband back from service overseas. He let him have the empty flat in town. I would have let him stay here but my husband was against it,' she drawled. 'Can't think why,' she added with a knowing smirk.

Spence nodded thoughtfully.

'Can you tell me where he is now?'

'I can't. I don't know. He's travelling around.'

'Why did he discharge himself from the hospital?'

'Dunno. I expect he felt capable and didn't want to waste any more of his leave in there.'

'Has he had the stitches out? Isn't he in pain?'

She shrugged. 'I expect he knows what he's doing.'

Spence wondered if he did.

'Is he regularly in touch with you?'

'Not regularly, but frequently. I spoke to him two days ago.'

'If he contacts you, tell him I need to see him urgently. What car is he driving?'

'A silver-grey VW Passat. Number N523 CWE.'

Spence wrote it down on the back of an envelope.

'Tell him I want to see him. Urgently!'

THIRTEEN

Gold followed him into the office.

'The super wants to see you urgently, sir.'

Spence groaned and made the face he reserved for Cherie Blair when he saw her on TV. 'What's he want, lass?'

'Didn't say. But he *did* say as soon as you come in.'

He nodded, threw off his raincoat and tramped down the corridor to the superintendent's office. He knocked on the door, opened it and looked in.

'Come in, Spence,' Superintendent Marriott squeaked. 'Come in and sit down.'

Spence sat down on the chair by the desk.

'Now then, lad, what's happening? Just checking up we are getting value for money. No arrest yet?'

'No.'

'How are you getting along with that landlord? The man that owns Kass's flat.'

'Symington … Can't find him, sir. Can't get hold of him. He's travelling round. Never at home. Harder to see than a dentist.'

'What's he up to?'

'Don't know, sir. Never in. Wife's no help. She knows nothing or she's fabricating. Just come back from there. I was about to alert traffic division, nationally. Got his car number and description.'

'Do that. And put all notifications to your own mobile, unless you're too important now to work unsocial hours. You won't get paid any more. The rate's the same.'

Spence shook his head. 'No. I'd already decided to do that, sir.'

'Is Symington your number one suspect?'

'Could be. There's more than him, though. Kass was quite a womanizer. He chased anything *married* in a skirt. He's initiated a lot of jealous feelings since he arrived in Castlecombe.'

'Hmmm. Any progress on that number? What was it – 122?'

'No, sir.'

'You've deliberately held it back?'

Spence nodded.

'Maybe it's time to make it known?'

'No. I'm not giving away any free information.'

Spence watched Marriott go through his repertoire of facial expressions, then revert to the usual look of an orang-utan.

'But we can't let this drag on.'

Spence rubbed his chin, then knowingly said, 'It won't drag on.'

Spence arrived at the office at 8.30 a.m. on Monday, 22 December 2003, which was the shortest day of the year and was, as forecast, cloudy and gloomy. He had spent all day Saturday and most of Sunday closeted in the box room, working on his new book. He would have completed a chapter were it not for Irene, who had called up and demanded he go downstairs to help her with the Christmas trimmings, which he did without much grace. He couldn't see the point as they were not expecting any visitors. Anyway, by teatime, the hall and the tree looked appropriately festive and Irene had a smile on her face, so he felt he had achieved something.

Before leaving the station on Friday afternoon, he had instructed Gold to request all forty-three police forces to inform him on his mobile number of any sighting of Symington's car. Consequently, during his long spells at the computer keyboard that weekend, he had been in constant expectation of the phone ringing, but it had been conspicuously silent. To say that he was disappointed was putting it mildly.

He switched on the light and began to unbutton his coat. He sniffed. The stuffy smell of warmed-up, reconstituted dust assaulted his nostrils, so he turned to open the office window. It was then that he heard the muffled, tinny sound of the mobile phone from his pocket. The first time he had heard it in three days. His pulse-rate quickened, and a lump in his chest started up and throbbed like a Flymo. He turned back from the window, dug into his pocket, pulled out the phone, opened the flap and pressed the button.

'This is Acting DI Spence,' he said crisply.

'Nottingham Central here. You were wanting info on a Passat?'

'Yes. Go ahead, please.'

'A motor patrol team on the A1 report sight of this car travelling at approximately sixty miles an hour northwards on the A1 on the stretch of dual carriageway north of Blyth near the county border. It is being driven by one IC male. The patrol still have eyeball. Do you want them to stop the driver?'

'No. No. Don't stop the car. Thank you very much. When was this call timed?'

'8.28. That's two minutes ago.'

'Great. Thank you very much indeed.'

He pressed the cancel button decisively, thrust the phone into his pocket, snatched open the door and started determinedly down the corridor. This was the news Spence had been waiting for: the opportunity to interview Edmund Symington. This man should be able to progress the enquiries substantially. A few questions would surely put him in the frame or eliminate him. He passed the female locker room, Gold was just coming out.

'Get your coat and meet me in the car park quickly. Hurry up!'

She stared at him. There was no time to reply. He had gone.

She turned back into the locker room, grabbed her navy-blue waterproof coat and chequered hat, ran down the corridor, past the cells and out of the back door.

Spence had already got the engine started and had the car facing the exit. He leaned over and opened the passenger door. She dived in.

Spence let in the clutch.

'You've heard from traffic, sir?' she said, stabbing in the seatbelt.

'Symington's on his way home ... I hope. We should get to his house before he does. Best time he could make would be about twelve minutes: we can be there in five or six.'

Spence raced his car out of Castlecombe on the road north to Darlington then he turned off on the Goathland road at the crossroads, over Rabbitspaw Bridge and up Hare lane on the Whitby road, and arrived outside Symington's house in record time. He slowed the car and drove unhurriedly between the stone pillars, up the drive, and across the front of the house, hoping that Mrs Symington had not seen them. He was a bit red in the face and he had a very slight tremor in his arms and hands. According to his conservative calculations, they were still three or four minutes ahead of him. He pointed the bonnet towards the pine trees and began to pull hard on full lock to the left as the first stage in turning the car round. He intended backing up to the trees so that he would have some cover and more easily be able to see Symington arrive. He planned to drive behind him and thereby cut off his retreat. However, it was at that moment, in his mirror, he saw the bonnet of a silver-grey Passat nose up to the front of the house. In the driver's seat was a man with a tanned face and fair hair.

'He's here, sir!' Gold yelled elatedly.

Spence was delighted. His assumption that Symington had been heading home had been correct.

'Good.' He nodded and sighed.

He had engaged the reverse gear to begin to move the car backwards when he heard the roar of an engine. The Passat appeared in his rear mirror, passed the back of his car, turned, drove over the lawn and disappeared down the drive and out through the stone pillars.

'He's seen us and he's off!' Gold shouted in alarm.

Spence's lips tightened. He thought something illegal, impossible and unprintable, and let in the clutch. The car leaped backwards, made a noise of protest and stalled. He turned the ignition key and restarted the engine. This time, he let the clutch in more gently. The car swerved backwards, making a hard curve. Then he slammed the gear stick into first gear and they were off, past the front of the house, down the drive. At the stone pillars, he had to stand on the brakes to stop for a lady pushing a buggy with a child in it. When the buggy was in the middle of the entrance to the drive, the child threw Mr Wibbly Wobbly out on to the tarmac. The mother saw it, slowly retrieved it and waved it, gently chiding at the child.

Spence winced.

Symington's car was not to be seen.

Gold yelled, 'He's getting away, sir!'

The mother waved the doll at the child. The child put its arms out to receive it.

Spence wanted to bang on the horn, but he didn't.

'Shall I get out? Move her on?' asked Gold.

'No! She'll go ...'

The mother was undecided: it seemed she was considering whether there was any point in giving the toy to the child for it to throw it out again.

'Pip your horn, sir.'

'No.'

Eventually a solution was reached: the mother resolved she would carry Mr Wibbly Wobbly in her shopping bag. She unhooked it from the buggy handle, took out her handbag, put the toy in the shopping bag and replaced the handbag on top of it. Then she looked back and saw that she was holding up Spence's car. She smiled, waved her thanks and pushed the pushchair along and out of their path.

Gold waved back.

Spence let in the clutch and surged into the road. There was no sign of the Passat and he didn't know which direction Symington had taken. He guessed it would be towards Castlecombe, so he turned right and pressed the car hard. Symington must be more than a quarter of a mile ahead by now. For the next five minutes, he whizzed along the road at speeds of up to sixty miles an hour. It was pretty wild along that narrow, high-hedged country road. He raced down Hare Lane, bounced over the brow of Rabbitspaw Bridge, round the corner and then suddenly, 300 yards ahead, he was surprised to see the Passat. He thought Symington might have put a mile or more between them; he had certainly had the opportunity if he had been hell bent on getting away. Spence pressed down on the accelerator and, after half a minute or so, was within a few yards of the Passat's rear bumper, then he flashed his lights and pipped his horn until the driver switched on his left indicator light and pulled up at the side of the road.

Spence sighed as he pulled on the handbrake. 'Be careful, lass. He might be dangerous.'

He leaped out of the car and sped up to the offside window of the Passat, while Gold made for the nearside.

Symington remained in the driver's seat and lowered the window. Spence looked him over warily. He was a wiry, athletic-looking man in his forties with a desert suntan.

'Good morning, sir. Are you in a hurry?'

Symington noticed Gold out of the corner of his eye, glanced at her and then turned back to look at Spence. He didn't reply.

'Are you Captain Symington?'

'Yes. Are you the police?' he said evenly.

'I am Acting Inspector Spence. I want to ask you some questions in connection with the murder of Ronald Kass. Will you accompany me to the station?'

'Well, I hardly know the man, but yes, of course.'

'Will you turn the ignition off, sir, and give me the keys?'

'Very well,' he said quietly and passed him the keys.

'We'll go in my car, if you don't mind. I'll get someone to bring your car in.'

Spence stepped back a few paces.

'Now if you would get out of the car?'

He watched as Symington struggled out of the seat, holding his stomach and leaning forward.

'Put your hands on the roof of the car.'

Symington's eyebrows shot up.

'What's all this?'

'Hands on the roof, sir. Thank you. Anything sharp in your pockets?'

'No,' Symington bawled. 'Of course not.'

Spence frisked him and found nothing hard and bulky. 'Thank you. Now if you'd get in my car.'

Spence noticed that he hobbled around, leaning slightly forward and still holding the lower part of his stomach. His face indicated that he appeared to be in pain.

'We'd better have you straight off to hospital,' Spence said.

'It's just some stitches need taking out. They've tightened up considerably.'

'Yes. I heard about that.'

Spence ushered him into the front passenger seat and closed the door. He then moved away from the car, turned to Gold and quietly said, 'I'll take him to the hospital in my car.'

She looked alarmed. 'On your own, sir?'

'It's all right. He can't run far. Get a patrol car to meet me at the hospital to take charge of him, and ask SOCO to collect *his* car for examination. And stay here with it until they arrive.' He handed her the keys. 'All right?'

'Right, sir,' she said but she wasn't altogether happy.

She glanced back at the man's tanned face looking at her through Spence's car windscreen. He made her feel distinctly uncomfortable. She reached into her pocket for her mobile.

It was not until after lunch that Symington was brought back to the station from the hospital. He had a brief private meeting with his solicitor, Miss Keys, a crisply dressed young woman in a dark suit, before being shepherded into the interview room by Gold.

Symington was still walking with difficulty. The hospital had provided him with an adjustable aluminium walking stick, which he leaned on when walking and standing.

Spence came in, nodded at Miss Keys and then looked across at Symington. 'I hope you feel more comfortable now?'

'Yes. Thank you, Inspector. They said I would be perfectly all right in a few days.'

'Good. Good. Will you sit down there, please, Mr Symington? Miss Keys, next to him. What is your full name, sir?'

'Edmund Symington,' he replied and shuffled into the seat.

Spence switched on the tape.

'Interview with Edmund Symington, 22 December, 1405 hours. Present, Miss Keys, WPC Gold and Acting Inspector Spence.'

Gold pulled out her notebook and held her pen at the ready.

'Yes now, Mr Symington, I've been trying to contact you since finding the body of Ronald Kass,' Spence said. 'What can you tell me about him?'

'Very little. He was a private in the army ... that's about all I know.'

'So you didn't *know* him?'

'Well, hardly.'

'He was almost a stranger to you?'

'Yes.'

Spence looked at him ruefully.

'He was in the same regiment as you, the same unit as you. You were his commanding officer,' Spence said irritably.

'Yes, well, so were 250 other men.'

Symington pursed his lips, looked at Miss Keys and then added, 'He worked in the HQ of the unit where I was stationed in Iraq. He was a clerk dealing with the ordering and storing of foodstuffs, as well as equipment such as field cooking ovens, refrigeration units and kitchen utensils.'

'How long had you known him?'

'I didn't *know* him. I came across him in the course of my duties. That's all.'

'You wouldn't have invited him to your house, then?'

'Good Lord, no,' Symington replied decisively, then switched on an easy smile.

Spence leaned forward and peered into his face.

'But you *did*, according to your wife. That's how *she* met him.'

The smile went. His eyes widened. His hands tightened.

'Oh. Well, yes. But that was only ... when he arrived ... the first night.'

'Tell me how you came to invite him up to Castlecombe ... and install him in your flat?'

'I didn't *install* him. He was among a small number of men who had come to the end of their term of duty and were being discharged. It is customary for the CO to show an interest in the welfare of his men and I asked him where he wanted his train pass to. It turned out he hadn't any family or anywhere particular to go. I asked him about employment – he hadn't a job to go to either. So ... I ... I knew I had a flat unoccupied and I thought he'd get a job up here easily enough. It seemed a good idea at the time.'

'So you were getting to like Kass, then?'

'He was pleasant enough. He was a young man at a loose end, that's all.'

'You must have known him pretty well. His mobile phone

records show he phoned your house phone four times after he arrived in Castlecombe.'

Symington blinked. His lips moved but he said nothing. That was clearly something he didn't know or hadn't expected Spence to know.

'Did you know he had a police record with a list of offences as long as your arm?' Spence said bluntly.

Symington's mouth dropped open. 'No,' he said, sounding shocked. 'Really? I didn't know,' he added.

Spence eyed him carefully and rubbed his chin. He thought he was a dreadful actor. He wouldn't even have cast him as *third* shepherd.

'As his CO, you would have had access to his records.'

Symington didn't reply.

'In his belongings, we didn't find a rent book,' Spence continued. 'How much rent did he pay you?'

'He hadn't paid anything. We hadn't discussed it. It would have been the going rate.'

'Did you row with him about it?'

'It was never discussed.'

'Or did you row about something else? His interest in your wife, for instance?'

Symington breathed in and then out slowly. 'He wasn't interested in my wife,' he replied quietly. 'Anyway, she wouldn't have been interested in him.'

'Oh? I thought, as *you* weren't aware of the phone calls, then the calls must have been made *to* your wife without you—' Spence broke off.

'What are you getting at?'

Spence didn't reply. He just looked at him.

Symington thought a moment, then glanced at Miss Keys, then Gold and then back at Spence, searching their faces to try to find out what each might be thinking.

Spence was well satisfied with himself. He was wickedly good at sowing seeds of distrust. 'Nothing,' he said nonchalantly. 'Nothing. What did you do before you joined the army?'

'I was a chef. I ran a restaurant.'

'You did all your own food preparation?'

'Yes. Cooked and prepared everything fresh myself.'

'Well used to carving, and boning joints and so on?'

'Oh yes,' Symington replied confidently.

'So you would know how and where to stick a knife then, wouldn't you?'

Symington's eyes flashed. 'Really!' he said angrily, and looked at Miss Keys.

The woman looked over her horn-rimmed spectacles, shook her head and said, 'Inspector, that's a wholly improper question.'

Spence appeared to think about it for a moment, nodded and said, 'Mmm. It is. Quite right. I withdraw it.'

Symington leaned back in the chair.

'It wasn't really a proper question, Mr Symington, I agree,' said Spence. 'It was really a statement. I have just found out Kass was murdered with a small bladed knife ... like an ordinary kitchen knife!'

'Well, that's awful, but it wasn't me,' he said. 'I've nothing against the man.'

'The knife pierced the aorta. It made a lot of blood. The murderer would have been quite heavily marked. Blood would have spurted out all over under pressure. There would have been blood everywhere, on the sleeve and down the front of the shirt or coat ... possibly even dripping down on to the shoes.'

Symington stared at him and shook his head.

Spence kept up the pressure. 'Hmmm. I went to your

house the day we found Kass's body. I was looking for you. In fact, I have spent eight days looking for you. In cases like this, those closest to the murdered person usually come forward and make themselves known. In your case you ran off and left no address where you could be contacted.'

Symington didn't reply. He continued staring ahead.

'Anyway, as I said, I went to your house. It was exceedingly windy and cold but there was a fire in the incinerator in the garden. Your wife said she was burning garden rubbish. On a wild day like that! *I suggest that she was disposing of your blood-soaked clothes.*'

'No.'

'While you were probably upstairs, hiding in the bedroom.'

'No. I was away.'

'Where?'

'Whatever I say, you won't believe me.'

'Try me.'

He didn't reply.

'Where were you on the evening of Monday 15th December, last Monday?'

'In hospital. I had had my appendix taken out. You *know* that.'

'No. You had discharged yourself the day before, on the Sunday.'

Symington looked down at his hands, shrugged and said, 'Well, then, I don't know.'

'Were you afraid that while you were on your back in hospital, your wife was having an affair with Kass, so you discharged yourself, still with your stitches in, to put an end to it and murder him?'

'No. No. Certainly not,' he said angrily.

'Where were you from the time you discharged yourself

from hospital a week yesterday, Sunday, until I stopped you this morning on the Whitby Road? That's eight days ... eight vital days.'

'No comment.'

'Were you hiding away to avoid being questioned by the police?'

'No comment.'

Spence leaned back in the chair, took in a deep breath, held it a second then pursed his lips and slowly blew it out. 'Very well.' He stood up. He turned to Gold.

'Arrest him. Charge him with murder. Get some temporary clothes for him and arrange for the clothes he's wearing to go to forensics.'

Gold felt a shiver run down her spine.

FOURTEEN

'Come in,' he called.

Gold came into the office with a cream file about an inch thick.

'Have SOCO gone to Symington's house?' he said.

'Yes, sir.'

'Good.'

Spence noticed the file in Gold's hand. 'What's that, your expense chittys?'

'Just come in from forensics, sir. For you.'

'What? All that lot?' Is it all re Kass?'

'Yes, sir. Pretty thorough, eh?'

'We'll have to see.'

He pointed to the desk and she placed the file in front of him.

He quickly opened it.

Gold made for the door.

'Hmmm. Just a minute,' said Spence.

She looked back.

'You realize that to convict Symington, we will have to link the number 122 to him? It's in the evidence – the stuff that's gone up to the CPS.'

She nodded.

'The army is full of numbers: his army number, unit

number, room number, vehicle number, locker number, passport number, to mention a few. Symington must have a connection directly with a 122 that Kass knew about. See what you can dig up. We have made such a point about it. We won't be able to get a conviction if we can't come up with a logical explanation for it.'

'Right, sir.'

'And get those 100 dinar notes from forensics and take them round to a bank. Any bank except the Northern,' he said, as he turned over a page. 'Find out what they're worth.'

'Were there any fingerprints on them, sir?'

'Only Kass's. Go on. Chop chop.'

'Right sir,' she said, reaching out for the door.

'Something else. While you're down there, bring Kass's socks back here. The ones he was wearing.'

'Socks?' she said, wrinkling up her nose.

He looked up and caught her reaction.

'They'll be in a plastic bag!' he bawled.

Spence strolled into Castlecombe House Hotel, through the new automatic doors into the posh foyer. He was taken aback by the Christmassy scene. The whole area was a fantasy of coloured foil trimmings, shimmering from the ceiling and walls, overwhelming everywhere except the bottom of the stairs, the lift entrance and the reception desk. On his left was a richly decorated Christmas tree laden with glittery boxes and twinkling coloured lights. He smiled as he surveyed this carnival feast for the eyes and listened briefly to 'Jingle Bells', which he thought was being rendered at incredible speed by a choir of castrated ferrets who'd been at the sherry. He sniffed as he registered that it was a timely reminder that the expensive excesses of the festive season were almost upon him.

He glanced towards the reception desk but there was nobody in sight. Surprising, he thought, only three days from Christmas. He pushed the side door into his favourite little bar. The only customer he could see was the unsavoury little man, the one who was always there. He was sitting at a little table by the door, as usual, guarding a glass of some dark liquid. Spence recalled that the scruff had introduced himself to him last time they met and he struggled to recall his name.

'Good afternoon, Mr Spence,' the little man said and held up his glass.

Spence lifted his hand in reply. 'Good afternoon, Mr erm …'

'Tripp, sir. Tripp it is.'

'That's right, of course. Good afternoon, Mr Tripp,' he replied, trying to feign camaraderie but making a bee-line for the bar.

The young man in the smart blue and black suit with the red dickie bow popped up from behind the pump handles with a smile as big as a piano keyboard.

'Nice to see you again, Mr Spence, sir. Is it still white wine and lemonade, with ice?'

'Aye, why not?' Spence said, hoisting himself on to a stool.

The barman pushed a glass under a box of wine and turned the tap.

'How's the writing going, sir?' the young man said, trying to show an interest.

Spence pursed his lips. 'Slow, lad. Slow. *Very* slow.'

'Sorry to hear that, sir. What's the trouble? Have you got that … what do they call it … that writer's block?'

'No. No, lad. Just not got the time.'

'Of course, you're helping out the police, aren't you?' the young man said as he put a pretty coaster with a rose decoration on it in front of the big man, and then put a long glass on top of it.

'Well, sort of.'

He slapped a £5 note on the bar.

'Thank you, sir.'

He didn't get much change. He looked down at it, grunted and picked it up.

'I read somewhere, Mr Spence, that your book was being translated and printed in *five* other languages. Is that right?'

'Not sure exactly how many, but yes, that sounds about right, lad, why?'

The young man's eyes widened.

'Do you get paid for those as *well*?'

Spence stared at him meaningfully. 'I should hope so,' he said with a sniff. 'Is Mr Hoffman about anywhere?'

'He *was* in the kitchen, sir. I think he's in reception at the moment.'

'Right,' Spence said, and he picked up the glass and slid off the stool. 'I'll see if I can find him. Thank you.'

He wandered out of the bar, through the foyer and up to the reception desk.

Mr Hoffman appeared as if by magic through a door behind the counter. He was wearing a big white hat and a big wide smile.

'Ah, Mr Spence, our celebrated author. You wanted to see me?' He grinned. 'You want me in one of your books?'

Spence managed a smile. 'One day, perhaps, Mr Hoffman. One day. At the moment, I'm just making an enquiry.'

'Ah yes. What can I help you wiz?'

Spence put his glass on the counter. 'Two weeks ago, Tuesday, 9th December, you had a party of three men staying here, I believe. Three men—'

'You are talkink like a policeman again.'

'I am a policeman again.'

Hoffman dropped the smile.

'Oh. Really? Congratulations. Three gentlemen on 9th December.'

'Yes. I am making some enquiries. You can help me—'

'Oh dear. I look here,' he said and turned back the pages of a big complicated book on the desk top. He ran his finger down a column. 'Tuesday, 9th December. Hmmm. There was no booking in the same name for sree men that night. We were fully booked, of course. They were mostly for single rooms – business men, salesmen. Some couples. Some double rooms let as single, but no ...'

Spence suddenly remembered and pointedly asked, 'Do you have a room number 122?'

'No. We only have thirty-six letting rooms,' Hoffman replied still checking off the bookings plan. 'Oh! I tell a lie. There was one double room, let as a single, but not paid for ... number twelve, in fact. The man, as I remember, cancelled the room at the last minute because he had to leave for ... somewhere, Atlantic City in the States, I think he said. Had a meal in the restaurant, though. Yes, he had the speciality of the house: trout à la maison. I remember because he was very complimentary about it. The nicest trout he had ever tasted in five continents, he said. He was wiz two other men. Yes. That would be the sree! I remember they left very suddenly ... very suddenly indeed. Yes. It was very strange.'

'Do you know who they were? Could you describe them to me?'

'Oh no, Inspector. Just average men. Not tall. Not short. Not fat. Not thin. The nice man was ... His name is in ze book, but crossed out. I can make it out. It is Basil Van de Meyer.'

'Basil Van de Meyer?' Spence was surprised and amused.

'Anuzzer ruddy foreigner,' Hoffman chuckled. 'Now *he* wore a very good suit, Mr Spence. Woollen, hand-woven material, I remember. Very unusual. And that watch on his wrist cost him more than twenty thousand francs!'

Spence shook his head in amazement.

'You know him?' Hoffman enquired, smiling.

'Not personally, no. But whenever Basil Van de Meyer has been around, Mr Hoffman, hoteliers don't have to bother taking stock of their towels and cutlery. Oh no. No. They have to check that anybody *he's* been in contact with has still got their necessary eight pints of blood!'

Spence went straight home and into the little box room where his computer was set up. He looked in his address book for a particular telephone number and dialled it on the bedroom extension.

There was a click and a gruff voice said, 'Yes?'

Spence said, 'Is that Andrew?'

'Might be.'

'Are you still with Antiques and Works of Art?'

'Might be.'

'It's Frank Norman Spence of Castlecombe CID. Remember me?'

The voice thawed. 'You old scallywag. Yes, of course I remember you, Frank. I thought you dropped one, wrote a book about it and were now full-time at home counting the money.'

'No. Not quite as simple as that. Working at the factory part-time. Are you still sergeant?'

'Chief Inspector Walker, Frank, if you don't mind. Now, what can I do for you?'

'Yes, indeed. I've had Basil Van de Meyer on my patch. Are you still interested in him?'

'Basil! We're always interested in Basil. He's been very quiet of late. What's he up to?'

'I have no idea. That's why I'm phoning you.'

'I could come up, very discreetly, if it's worth my while, Frank?'

'No. No. Don't do that. He's not here now. No idea where he is, or the identity of who he saw. He visited – didn't even stay – in a local hotel, that's all I know. Just want to keep my finger on the pulse, Andrew. What sort of thing would bring him out of the woodwork, especially up here in the sticks?'

'I don't know. Any sort of big-time lucre. Gold, diamonds, jewels. I must say, these days, he's unlikely to look at anything under a million quid.'

'Thought so. Are *you* looking for anything at the moment that he might be fishing around for?'

Walker thought for a moment; it was not the sort of question a policeman would normally ask *or answer* other than only to another policeman he trusted. 'The Baverstock diamonds?'

'Never heard of them. Anything else?' Spence replied.

'The Persian Salamander?'

'Good morning, sir.'

'Good morning, lass. Come in. What do you want?'

'While you were out yesterday afternoon, I went round all the shops on the High Street, sir. Nobody has any CCTV that covers the pavement.'

'Right,' Spence said, taking off his coat.

'And as we hadn't heard, I phoned SOCO's office to find out about that footprint in the sugar at that café. It's a man's shoe.'

'I'm not on *that* case.'

'No, sir,' she said. 'And I had another email from South

Yorkshire police to say that a retail grocers in Doncaster was broken into two nights back ... with the usual messing around with the sugar. Nothing taken.'

Spence looked at her thoughtfully.

'Hmmm. Interesting.' Then he added, 'But I'm *not* on that case!'

'No, sir. Also, the CPS have got some notes for you about Symington's evidence.'

He pulled a face. 'I bet they have!'

He looked down on his desk. He saw a polythene evidence bag. He could see what was in it without even opening it: a pair of red woollen socks. He passed the bag back to her.

'What's the matter, sir? Don't you want these now?'

'Have those socks been darned?' he asked.

She took the bag from him. 'It looks like it to me, sir. Yes. Yes, they certainly have. And a much better job than I could have done. I personally wouldn't have bothered. You can buy socks, better than those, for a pound a pair.'

His eyes lit up.

'Ah,' he said, as if he had just discovered the meaning of life. '*There's* the difference between the generations. You *wouldn't* have considered darning them, my wife *may* have darned them and my mother *definitely* would have! The woman who darned those socks is more likely to be over forty than under thirty. Hmmm. That definitely rules out Mrs Lee.'

'I thought Symington murdered Kass, sir. If he did, what does it matter *who* darned the socks?'

Spence looked straight at her.

'All will be revealed, when *you* find out the significance of the number 122. Don't you see? We have this case built around Symington – motive, means and opportunity, which are all in place and a hundred per cent valid – *but* we haven't actually any hard evidence. *Nobody* witnessed the murder, *no* weapon has been found and linked to him and there's *no* supporting forensic of any kind. *And* the man hasn't even a record.'

The phone rang. He reached out for it.

'Spence,' he snapped into the mouthpiece. 'Yes, Ron?'

His eyes narrowed. His mouth dropped open and stayed open.

Gold noticed the change in him. He was upbeat again.

'Yes ... Buttons and zip and everything ... Right ... I understand that, Ron. Thanks very much.'

Spence's chest began to tingle.

He replaced the phone slowly and beamed up at her.

'That fire in the garden at Symington's?'

'Yes, sir.'

'I asked Ron Todd particularly to look in that incinerator. In the ashes they've found the buttons, zip and so on from a man's suit.'

She nodded appreciatively.

He squeezed an earlobe between finger and thumb. 'Of course, there's little or no chance of being able to detect the presence of any blood, but he said they'd try for it.'

Gold smiled and nodded enthusiastically.

Then she said, 'You see, sir. It's coming.'

He frowned. 'What?'

'Evidence, sir. It's coming.'

He pulled a face. 'Yes,' he growled and rubbed his chin. 'Like Christmas.'

Mrs Carrington, in a spotless white overall, her hair done up like a pineapple with straggles sticking out at the top, smiled sweetly at a little old lady, took her money and banged her fingers on the keys of the till. The bell rang and the drawer slid open. She pushed in a note and took out some coins. 'There you are, Mrs Morrison. And a Merry Christmas to you and Mr Morrison.'

'And to you, Mrs Carrington. Goodbye.'

The old lady fitted a loaf in her bag and made for the door. There were no other customers in the shop.

Spence moved up to the counter.

Mary Carrington saw him, looked dismayed for a second then switched on a smile, leaned forward and said, 'Well, it's our clever policeman and author, Mr Spence. And what can I do for you, Inspector?' she said, her eyelids flickering and her big smiling mouth twitching expectantly.

Spence pushed a hand into his raincoat pocket and pulled out the polythene evidence bag containing the pair of Kass's socks, which he placed neatly on the counter. 'Do you recognize these, Mrs Carrington?'

She pursed her lips, picked up the bag and held it up to the light. 'What is it, Mr Spence?'

He blew a silent whistle and waited.

Suddenly, there was a noise emanating from the door behind her. It flew open and a tray laden with bread, still steaming, arrived through it, followed by Russell Carrington, white-faced and perspiring. He didn't seem to notice Spence.

Mrs Carrington, still holding the evidence bag, turned round to face him.

'Russell!' she said, admonishing him. 'We have a visitor!'

He stopped in his tracks, looked round, saw Spence, nodded at him, licked his lips, lowered the tray on to the far end of the counter, then looked back at her.

'There's some custard tarts to come – they need to set a bit longer,' he said and made a dash for the door to the back.

'It's Mr Spence, Russell!' she said imperiously.

He stopped, turned back and looked at him momentarily.

'Hello,' he said sheepishly and wiped his perspiring hands down his white coat. Then he looked at his wife and observed that she was holding something. His eyes zoomed down to it like a cat to a goldfish. She noticed it had caught his attention, and dropped the bag on to the counter, put her hands down by her sides and looked away.

Russell Carrington lunged forward and grabbed it. He held it up and shook it vigorously. His face changed from sweaty pasty-white to sweaty scarlet.

'Yes! Yes! These are *his* socks,' he said, spraying saliva over Spence's new raincoat. He stepped back a pace. 'These are the socks she darned for him. That's proof positive!'

Mrs Carrington put her hands across her ears and shook her head.

'Shut up, Russell!' she screamed. 'Shut up! You don't know *what* you're saying!'

'Don't I?' he bawled. 'I saw you smarming and greasing all over him!' He threw the bag on the floor by Spence's feet, turned and rushed out through the door to the back of the shop and slammed it noisily behind him.

Mrs Carrington's face creased up as if she might cry.

The shop doorbell rang and a man came in.

Spence bent down, retrieved the evidence bag, put it in his pocket and then stepped away from the counter as the customer approached.

Mrs Carrington saw the customer, removed her hands from her ears, took a very deep breath, ran her hands down her bosom to smooth out non-existent creases, straightened the wrapping paper on the counter, switched on a smile and looked enquiringly across at the man. She maintained the smile throughout the simple transaction, which involved the exchange of a small brown loaf for money.

'And a Merry Christmas to you,' the gentleman said. The doorbell rang again and the door closed.

The smile vanished. She turned to Spence.

'Yes. I was the one that darned his socks,' she said angrily. 'And that's *all* I did. That Chinese woman from across the way there. She was always going up there supposedly delivering him hot takeaways, huh! She'd sometimes be a half-hour or more. You don't see *her* husband shouting and screaming at *her* ... even though, in her case, he'd probably have good cause! Now my husband seems to think that helping a young man along like that is a crime. He's just very jealous. He's always been like that. I sometimes think I won't be able to stand his jealous moods. It's times like these when I wish my dear mother was still alive. I would have happily nursed her and looked after her and stayed with her. Oh, I did love my mother. I'd have someone sympathetic to go to when I was depressed or in trouble. And I wouldn't have minded looking after her in her old age. It would have been a privilege. There are still people who respect the elderly, you know, Mr Spence. Like that man upstairs, that nice young man, Raymond Turvey. Runs after his mother, fetches and carries shopping, takes her to the hospital, nothing seems too much trouble for him. He calls and sees her a lot more since the murder – two or three times a day. Well, she must be nervous. Understandable. He must get special consideration from the bank. And she's a difficult old bat if ever I met one. She's never satisfied, always complaining. If I can't get that sort of devoted love and care and attention now, at my age, what hope is there for me when I get old?'

Spence rubbed his chin and smiled sympathetically.

'I'm sorry, Mr Spence, to moan at you like this,' she continued.

'That's all right.'

'I get very worried. And Russell is a bit backward, you know. He had a difficult childhood. His mother had big plans for him. He was her only child. She brought him up on her own. You *will* make allowances for him, won't you?'

FIFTEEN

'Oh, you're back, sir.'

'What is it, lass?'

'I took those 100 dinar notes to Barclays and to NatWest and they both said the same thing, sir. The stuff is just so much wastepaper.'

'Mmm. Confirms what Raymond Turvey said. At least we now know it didn't form any part in the motive for murdering Kass.'

'And I just heard a whisper that SOCO has found a trace of some white crystals or something in the boot of Symington's car.'

'Eh? Symington and drugs? How did you find that out? I haven't had a report, official or otherwise.'

'Bumped into Ron Todd in the canteen. It's not checked out, sir.'

'Hmmm.'

The phone rang. He reached out for it.

'Spence.'

'You'd better come down here.'

It was the superintendent. He didn't sound happy. He never did.

'Right, sir,' Spence said and replaced the phone.

'That's the super. He's going to tell me the case won't stick!'

Gold's face dropped.

'Oh, sir.'

'That's all right,' he said with a nod. 'It's given me the edge I needed.'

'What's that?'

He was down at the superintendent's door in a minute.

'Sit down. I've read the file and the CPS notes, and the case against Symington is not conclusive.'

'No, sir, but it fulfils the rules. He had the motive, opportunity and means.'

'What means?'

'An instrument with a point and a blade, sir. A kitchen knife, for instance.'

'Hmmm.' He turned over a page. 'The motive's clear enough. The victim was clearly a menace to every young woman he came in contact with—'

'And older women too. Mrs Symington was in her forties.'

'What's *she* say?'

'Knows nothing; denies everything.'

'And "opportunity"?'

'He says he wasn't there, but he can't or won't say *where* he was. He discharged himself from hospital with stitches still in him, the day *before* the murder, and he can't account for his movements for that day and the following five days.'

'Why would he do that? For six days? Amnesia?'

'No, sir. I don't know.'

The superintendent closed the file.

'We'll never get a conviction with a weak case like this. The CPS will insist on some indication of his actual or his claimed whereabouts at the time of the murder. You don't

even *attempt* an explanation. He may have been for an innocent week's holiday in … in Skegness.'

'If he had, he's had plenty of opportunity to say so, and I
am not allowed to use a thumbscrew.'

'Has he been to court?'

'Yes, sir. Charged. Bail requested and refused. He's on
remand here. Moving him to Wakefield SAP. They've no
room there. Could be after Christmas.'

The superintendent tossed the file to the end of the desk
and sniffed. 'If he's found guilty on the strength of *that*,' he
said, pulling a face like a monkey's backside, 'I shall reckon
you're getting your money under false pretences, *Agatha*!'

Spence came out of his office. He was neither surprised
nor disappointed. Strange though it may seem, everything
was going to plan. Spence's plan. But he didn't like Marriott's
attitude and he growled all the way up the corridor to his
office. 'Merry Christmas, huh!' He secretly hoped that
Marriott's turkey would be underdone and his sprouts would
be swimming in water.

He had not been offered another case so there was little for
him to do until the CPS had formally rejected the case against
Symington, which would certainly happen unless, of course,
there were any unexpected finds at Symington's house.

Spence considered bringing Mrs Symington into the station
and interviewing her but decided that it would likely be a waste
of time; he did not think she would give evidence *against* her
husband. The pressure was on Symington and that's where he
wanted it to be. The man was safe enough in the cells.

Spence reckoned his plan would hold.

He cleared his desk, had a pie and a Christmas drink with
Gold at the Fat Duck, went home and got back to writing his
novel.

*

Christmas 2003 came and went.

Spence got another knitted cardigan he didn't like, didn't fit, and he didn't want. It was wrapped around a bottle of Famous Grouse, which was OK. He gave Irene a cheque, which suited her very well. And their nephews and nieces all got useful cheques.

On the day itself, they had turkey followed by plum pudding, listened to the Queen's speech, watched *It's a Wonderful Life* on television, supped a bottle of champagne, slept through *The African Queen* and before you could say 'personal loan', Christmas 2003 was over.

Spence had spent most of the three-day break upstairs in the little box room banging away at his computer, hacking away at his second novel, hoping and praying it was going to be at least as good as *Scatter My Ashes*.

It was ten o'clock on Saturday, 27th December, and he was wrestling with a knot in the plot that was trying his patience, when Irene came into the room with a beaker of tea and a letter just delivered by the postwoman.

He looked up. For once, he welcomed the interruption.

'Letter from your agent,' she said, handing it to him and placing the beaker on an AOL installation disk he used as a coaster.

'Thanks, love,' he said, and took his hand off the mouse to take the envelope.

'You haven't forgotten you're taking me to the hair-dressers this morning, have you?' she said.

'No,' he lied, slitting open the letter with a penknife. 'What time have you to be there?'

'In an hour.'

'Right,' he said, unfolding the expensive cream letterhead and discarding the envelope. His eyebrows shot up. 'Hey. Listen to this.'

'Don't let your tea go cold.'

Spence read: 'I am pleased to advise that we have sold the rights on your behalf, to translate and print *Scatter My Ashes* to the leading publisher in Czechoslovakia, and that payment will be made to you in the next few days.'

'Oh.' Irene smiled. 'That's good news, Frank.'

'Yes,' he said beaming. 'Fancy, Czechoslovakia. It's fantastic. Fancy them wanting to read my book in Czechoslovakia. All those 'z's, 'c's and 't's. Hmmm. It won't be much money, Irene. After all, Czechoslovakia is only a small country.'

'Yes, but it's good, isn't it? And it's all money in the bank, Frank!'

'Yes,' he chuckled. 'Mustn't look a gift horse and all that.'

'Hurry up, love, and get ready.'

'Yes,' he said. He began to close the computer down. 'Tell you what, Rene. I feel like celebrating. I could go up to Castlecombe House. I could knock a few bottles about. You take the car. Drop me off and you can pick me up later, after you've had your hair done, and join me there for lunch.'

She wasn't too pleased with that idea. He wouldn't drive the car once he had had a drop past his lips; *she'd* have to do the driving and find a place in town to park. Also, it sounded as if he intended to have *more* than a drop or two! Anyway, hell, it was Christmas, so just before eleven o'clock, she delivered him to the front door of Castlecombe House Hotel.

He made his way through all the wafting trimmings into the small bar, where the little man who was always there looked up at him. Spence searched his memory for his name, remembered it and even smiled down at him.

'Good morning, Mr Tripp.'

'Good morning, Mr Spence. Did you have a nice Christmas?'

'Indeed I did.'

He pulled the stool up to the bar and banged the palm of his hand lightly on the bar.

'Where's that chirpy barman?'

A head popped up between two pump handles.

'I'm here, Mr Spence. I'm here. Compliments of the season to you. You sound full of it this morning.'

'I am. I am. And the season's compliments to you, lad. I'll have a pint of Old Peculier, if you please.'

'Certainly, sir,' he said, selecting a glass.

'And give Mr Tripp here a pint of whatever he's supping, and have one yourself.'

'Oh. You're very kind, Mr Spence. Mine's a Guinness, if you please,' said the little oily man, Tripp, from behind.

'I'll have a half of bitter, thank you,' the barman said.

Spence nodded, smiled and looked round.

The barman said, 'Haven't seen anything of you over Christmas.'

'No. Been at home. Didn't want to turn out … bother the relations. You can't know what the weather's going to do.'

'Busy writing, I expect. How's it going?'

'Slow. Slow. It's always slow. Have you got a paper?'

The barman slapped a newspaper on the bar. 'There you are, sir.'

'Mmmm. See what's on the telly tonight.'

Spence glanced at the front page. The heading of a small item at the bottom of a column caught his eye.

Ten Million Reward for Salamander

The new Department of Treasures and Antiquities circular offers a reward of ten million new dinar for information leading to the recovery of the Persian Salamander.

The jewel was thought to have been housed in a vault hidden in the Glass Palace, Baghdad, which was destroyed when the country was invaded early this year. The Persian Salamander was a gift from the late Shah's grandfather to the country of Iraq in 1884, and said to be beyond price. It comprises over eighty large old-cut diamonds and forty Burmese rubies set in lapis lazuli sculpted to represent a reptile.

Spence thought about the jewel for a moment and reflected briefly how much ten million new dinar might be in sterling. Sounded like a tidy sum. Even if he should come across the Salamander in the course of his investigations – and it *had* been mentioned to him a couple of times this past week – as a servant of the Queen he wouldn't be entitled to claim the reward. He shrugged, then turned over some more pages, looking for the programmes on the telly. His eye caught something unusual on the half-page devoted to *Public Notices*. It was the headline.

Short Notice Auction

On the instructions of the Ministry of Defence, at the Central Drill Hall, Lucknow Barracks, Sebastopol Road, Birmingham. 10 a.m., 2nd Friday, January 2004.

Surplus catering foodstuffs, food preparing machinery, field ovens, field refrigeration units, tools, spares, et cetera.

Also quantity in paper sacks of flour, currants, raisins, salt, cornflakes, sugar, porridge oats, tea, coffee, etc. Quantity in tins of corned beef, spam, dried egg, dried milk, dried custard, prunes, apricots, oranges, pears, marmalade, strawberry preserves. Also packeted chocolate. Quantity of ovens, pans, containers, tanks, refrigeration equipment, compressors, bottled oxygen, gas bottles, field ovens, ground stakes, mallets, tool kits, canvas screens, rope, oil, diesel containers, serving spoons, ladles, cutlery, etc. Some machinery and utensils unused, some very little used. Everything must go.

Auctioneers: F. Pullman & Sons Limited, Tavistock Road, Birmingham. No catalogues. Viewing morning of sale only. Doors open 7 a.m. Sale begins 10 a.m. Cash and approved cheques only.

Hmmm, he thought. Short notice auction ... now there's a thing.

A loud, friendly voice from behind disturbed him.

'Ah, Mr Spence, our local author.'

It was Mr Hoffman in a chef's hat peering through the door behind him.

'Have you dragged yourself away from your next verk of literature to be viv us today?'

'Good morning,' Spence said, lowering the newspaper and swivelling round on the stool. 'Belated Merry Christmas to you.'

'Tank you and to you.'

Hoffman suddenly came quickly into the room and across to him.

'I know not whether you intend staying for luncheon, but I have the most nicest, freshest, local trout on the menu,' he said enthusiastically. 'Now zat will be a change from ze turkey and roast potatoes, won't it?'

Spence smiled. 'Sounds very nice. Yes. I *would* like trout. Sounds very good.'

'It is. I promise. I am serving vis artichoke bottoms, and new potatoes ... to keep simple the flavours. You will see.'

He went out and closed the door.

'A glass of Old Peculier,' Spence called out to the little

barman, who nodded. Spence's phone began to ring. He
pulled the mobile out of his pocket and read the LCD. It was
Irene. He pressed the speak button.

'Yes, Rene. Are you looking all beautiful?'

'I'm done here, Frank,' she said in a businesslike voice.
'But I have just realized the sales are on.'

'What! Yes?' he said. He knew what was coming. 'You
want to miss lunch here, have a shufti round the shops and
pick me up later?'

'Yes. Is that all right?'

'Yes, all right, my love. Goodbye.'

'Goodbye.'

He closed the phone and dropped it into his pocket. He
swooped down on the ale in front of him, took a sip, slapped
some coins on the coaster where the glass had been, swivelled off the stool, and made his way down the length of the
reception hall, weaving round small groups of people
talking, and through the open double doors into the restaurant.

It was a small but immaculate dining room with only
twelve tables, covered with heavily starched, blindingly
white tablecloths, sparkling silver cutlery and glinting glass-
ware. Almost all the places were taken by other eager diners,
who must have been drinking and congregating in the main
bar. The waiter showed Spence to a small table set for one,
next to the wall. Spence declined a starter, ordered the trout
and another glass of Old Peculier.

In due course, the dish arrived covered with a silver lid
and a split tureen of vegetables. The waiter whisked off the
cover and disappeared. Spence soon cleared his plate and was
highly delighted with the trout. It really was most excellent.
The fish tasted rich and sweet, and he wondered what exotic
sauces, flavourings, herbs, wine and special cooking

Hoffman had applied to it to make it so magnificent. The flavours of the vegetables also had been heightened. Spence knew the Swiss were well regarded for their culinary skills and Hoffman had more than maintained their international reputation. Spence thought he would remember the taste of the trout for many years to come. He was disappointed that Irene had not been there to share the experience, but he resolved to return very soon and bring her with him.

He paid the bill, retired from the table, and, unusual for him, sent a glowing complimentary message written on a menu through to Mr Hoffman. He returned to the small bar, ordered a pot of coffee and had almost dropped asleep when Irene tapped him on the shoulder. It was almost four o'clock.

She took him home where he spent the next four days in the little box room, next to the bathroom, bashing out the novel. The occasional rattle on the windows of wind-driven hailstones and sight of the delicate sprinkling of snow on the pine trees, the lawn and the fields beyond made the discipline seem idealistic. He kept his head down, breaking off only for cups of tea and meals. He had made good, slow progress and was generally pleased with the way the story was developing and rolling out so smoothly.

On occasional moments, when his eyes were tired and he had reached a point where it was necessary to refresh himself with the plot outline, he leaned back in the chair and momentarily the spell left him. It was then that he began to wonder why he hadn't heard from Superintendent Marriott. Christmas was always a notoriously busy time for criminal activity, including serious crime, and he was not a little miffed that he had not been offered another commission. Also, unless anything significant had been discovered by SOCO at Symington's house, or the sprinkle of white stuff in the man's car boot turned out to be an illegal substance, the CPS would definitely reject the case and he would be called back to the station. But there had been absolute silence. And he wondered why. He was tempted to phone Gold. She might know what was going on. He was thinking about that when Irene popped in with a cup of tea. He asked her what she thought. She was in no doubt about what he should do. She encouraged him to continue writing and to take advantage of the free time while it was there. The force would get in touch with him soon enough. She was right there. The CPS were bound to come back – he knew that. The white powder in the boot of Symington's car could put an entirely different complexion on the case.

SIXTEEN

'I tell you what, Irene, it's New Year's Day – let's have lunch at Castlecombe House. You can taste Hoffman's magnificent trout for yourself.'

Irene Spence was truly surprised. Her face brightened.

'What about your book?'

'I need a change.'

'All right, Frank. Sounds very nice,' she said with a smile. 'You've made quite a song and dance about that trout. But you mustn't have too much to drink.'

His eyes flashed.

'I *never* have too much to drink,' he growled and reached out for the phone. 'I'll book a table.'

Spence put on his best suit and his Christmas tie and looked very smart, while Irene put on the elegant two-piece she had bought the week before at the sales. They looked quite the dashing couple as they strolled into the little bar at the Castlecombe House Hotel.

The oily little man, Tripp, in his usual place, glanced at them.

'Morning, Mr Spence,' he said with a smile.

'Morning, Mr Tripp. This is my wife.'

He leered at her, waved an unwashed hand, then his wet, bleary eyes scanned her from the heels of her shoes to the top of her head and then smirked slyly at Spence as he looked back at him.

'Good morning, missus.'

Irene looked at him, frowned then smiled back accommodatingly.

The bar tender was at the ready.

'Happy new year, Mr Spence,' he said with a big smile. 'Would you like something to drink?'

Spence looked enquiringly at Irene.

'A tomato juice, Frank, please,' she said.

He nodded and pointed to an easy chair by the window.

'Happy new year, lad. And I'll have a glass of Old Peculier.'

The barman selected a glass, put it under the tap and began to pull the pump handle.

'I heard how you enjoyed that trout the other day. You made Mr Hoffman's Christmas. He was telling all the staff what you'd written. He said he'd never heard you say anything complimentary about his cooking – or about anything – before.'

Spence smiled. What he said may have been true.

'You don't need to say owt if it's as good as you expect,' he began quietly. 'And you get what you pay for,' he said, placing a £10 note on the bar. 'That trout last Saturday was exceptionally good … exceptionally good … and I *said* so, that's all.'

The waiter came into the bar and invited them to take their place in the restaurant. He put them at a table for two at the far end near the window. It was just as busy as it had been when he'd been there on his own on Saturday last.

When the trout came, his eyes lit up and he soon had his fork into the fish.

Irene was slower and more patient.

Spence chewed slowly on the trout and his face showed his disappointment.

Irene noticed.

'What's the matter?'

He shook his head and pulled a face.

'That's not it. It's not right,' he said.

He wrinkled his nose and placed the fork on the plate.

She looked concerned; her eyes said everything.

'Is it off?'

'No. Have a taste. Leave it if you don't like it.'

Irene selected a piece of the fish and delicately cut it away. She loaded it on to her fork and lifted it to her mouth.

Spence watched her carefully. She chewed the fish suspiciously, then her face relaxed and her eyes lit up. She smiled and said, 'It's beautiful. Absolutely beautiful. It's everything you said it was, Frank. Now what's the matter with yours?'

Irene was not one to say anything she didn't mean. Spence looked at her and frowned but didn't say anything. With a look and a gesture, she invited him to have a taste of hers.

He picked up his fork, clawed a piece of fish from her plate and passed it up to his mouth. Two chews, then he chased it round his mouth and swallowed it.

'There you are,' she said. 'It's imagination. It's beautiful. Now eat it while it's hot.'

He shook his head and wrinkled up his nose.

'No. It's *not* the same as I had last Saturday.'

'It's very nice … a beautiful flavour.'

He picked up his knife and fork and grudgingly began to eat it. 'It's not the same … nothing like the same. Nothing like as tasty. The fish was as fresh and sweet as it could be. Hoffman has definitely done something different to it. Something *very* different,' he added heavily.

Irene's jaw tightened. 'Oh, do get on with it. It's quite the nicest restaurant meal I've had in years.'

'When you prepare something to perfection, why change it?' Spence said, refusing to be silenced. 'That's modern thinking for you. Evolution. It's true in all walks of life. Grandfather creates something and works all his life to make it near perfect, his son spends his life improving it to make it *absolutely* perfect, then the grandson comes along and knocks it all down, replaces it with something inferior, made in China, at treble the price. Works half as well, for much less time, that nobody will service, nobody will repair ... You can't even *speak* to anybody about it – only press numbers on the phone pad and listen to incomprehensible bit-part players from the Royal Shakespeare Company. When faulty, you have to throw it out and buy another!'

Irene glared at him.

The row continued.

Angrily, Spence grudgingly paid the bill and swept out of the restaurant and the hotel. Irene felt she had no alternative but to accompany him. She would have enjoyed a sweet and a coffee and a sit down in the lounge for the meal to properly digest.

Twenty minutes later, they arrived home.

Irene was fuming. She said that Frank had done nothing but complain and had completely ruined the occasion.

He was equally angry and said that she had missed the point and not taken the matter at all seriously. He insisted that the trout was *not* as before. That's what he had ordered, and that's what he had expected! And he was *not* prepared to shrug it off.

He returned to his writing.

Irene busied herself in the kitchen then settled down with a good book.

The atmosphere was frosty in the Spence house that night.

It was almost eleven o'clock the following morning when Spence arrived at the reception desk counter at the Castlecombe House Hotel. He tapped the bell with the palm of his hand.

A few moments later, the big, smiling figure of Mr Hoffman in a chef's hat and coat came out of the kitchen. When he saw who it was, he frowned, advanced to the counter and said, 'Mr Spence? You want to complain? My waiter told me you no like the trout? Yet it was *beautiful* ... everybody say it was nice. I taste it myself. And *he* say you ate *every* morsel. What's the matter, Mr Spence? I don't understand. You had it last Saturday and said it was delightful, did you not say?'

'I want to apologize,' he said.

Hoffman smiled. 'No need to apologize. If you don't like my food, you don't like my food. But if I don't cook it right you must *say*. Now what was the matter wiz it?'

'My wife thought the trout was delightful. So did I.'

'But I thought—'

'The point I was trying to make was that it was not ... *not* the same as last Saturday, that's all.'

'What's that?'

'You didn't cook it the same as last Saturday.'

'But I did ... *in every particular!*' Hoffman said positively. 'Mr Spence, my family finds a particular way of cooking a dish that delights the palates of my customers, would I change it? Would I casually, needlessly, change a successful recipe that had been perfected through three generations? No.'

'I know you chefs have all sorts of mysterious secret herbs, spices and processes that maybe you don't want to talk about ...'

'Maybe. Maybe.'

'And you may have forgotten to—'

'No!' he bawled. 'I cook *all* ze food in this restaurant. I take personal responsibility for all the dishes. That trout yesterday made twelve servings and each serving was identically prepared and cooked. I repeat, identically prepared and cooked, as were all the portions served on Saturday last. On zat, I stake my reputation. I have no reason to lie, Mr Spence.'

That was true. He had no reason to lie. But nevertheless there was a striking difference in the taste. Spence wondered if he should put the mystery down to being just one of those things?

'Well, there *was a difference*,' Spence said firmly. 'A significant difference.'

'I don't see how. The trout came from the same supplier. Both fish were about the same weight and colour.' Hoffman stopped and looked pointedly at Spence. 'Come to think of it, I have heard that fish taste different that are caught in different locations. The difference of the salt in the water, temperature and so on, I suppose.'

Spence's eyebrows went up.

'Yes,' he replied thoughtfully. 'Well, who supplied you with the fish?'

Hoffman blinked and put his hand to his mouth and massaged his jaw. 'Now zat could be a difficult kvestion.'

Spence smiled.

'I am not a policeman any more, Mr Hoffman. I am retired. I have been engaged to solve a murder case. If a petty offence like poaching is involved, I wouldn't be interested in bringing a charge against anybody.'

He nodded knowingly.

'Please wait here. I won't be a minute.'

He turned and went through the door to the kitchen. He was gone about three minutes and then reappeared with the horrible little scruff from the small bar, Mr Tripp, who came sneakily through the door holding his glass in one hand and his cap in the other. Hoffman said: 'I have told this gentleman that you are not at all interested in bringing a case against him. Indeed, if there even is one, for poaching or anything else, and that you are solely interested in determining where the trout came from. Is zat correct?'

'Absolutely correct, Mr Tripp,' Spence said, beaming down at him.

Hoffman nodded. 'There you are, Mr Tripp. Now please tell Mr Spence what he wants to know. I must get on with my preparations. You'll excuse me.'

'Thank you, Mr Hoffman.'

The kitchen door closed.

'I tickled the trout out of the stream under the bridge at the bottom of Hare Lane that leads into Dingle pond, Mr Spence. They were big ones – it took some doing, you know. Lots of patience. Blocked them off with nets at both ends, you see. That's how I does it ...'

'And when did you actually catch the fish and deliver them to Mr Hoffman?'

'The first one on Saturday morning last, about nine o'clock,' Tripp said with a sniff. 'The other I caught forty yards further upstream ... I brought that here early on New Year's Day, about half-past nine.'

'So they were both taken out of the same stretch of water?'

'That's right.'

'And eaten same day as caught.'

'Yes. You can't get much fresher than that, Mr Spence!'

Spence nodded. But it still didn't explain the difference in the taste.

'What did you wrap them in?'

'Newspaper, what else?'

'And what did you carry them in?'

'Big canvas satchel ... used to be my father's.'

Spence shook his head. He was going nowhere. He was beginning to think that he had spent enough time trying to understand why the taste of fish from the same stream, cooked by the same chef in the same kitchen in the same way, tasted so different. He couldn't explain to himself why he persisted with this ... brain-teaser. He decided to let it be one of life's great unsolved mysteries. There are plenty of them. It didn't matter. And he felt an irresistible urge to return home: he had a book to write.

'Ah well. Thanks very much, Mr Tripp.'

'You're very welcome, sir.'

Spence turned away from the little man and went straight out of the hotel. He returned home, put the car in the garage, went into the house, and said very little to Irene – and she said very little back as he was not in her good books. He took off his coat, put on his slippers, went straight up to the little box room and switched on his computer.

Irene was still a bit miffed about the short-lived trip out to lunch of the previous day. She didn't refer back to it directly but she was still huffy. She still didn't understand what the fuss was all about. She couldn't see the point: she simply thought he was being difficult. She didn't understand that a simple but inexplicable mystery like a difference in the taste of fish caught and cooked in an identical way, was an unbearable aggravation to her husband, ex-detective and now top crime writer.

Spence settled down in front of the computer screen, waiting for it to load up, and was considering that there was a certain amount of time one should spend on any job. And he decided he had reached the limit. He considered other matters. He still hadn't heard from the station. He was almost desperate to phone Gold and see what was happening. In particular, he wanted to know what the white powder was that was found in the back of Symington's Passat.

As the computer programme opened, he settled himself comfortably in the chair and scrolled up to the page he wanted.

His own story was coming out quite well. He worked intensively through Friday afternoon and evening, then all day Saturday and the day following, until at four o'clock on Sunday afternoon he went downstairs because his eyes were tired. He slumped in the chair in the living room and watched *Songs of Praise* and *Summer Wine*, and then began to nod.

'Your dinner's ready, Frank.'

He heard Irene call, vaguely, in the distance, two or three times. He pulled himself together. He gripped the chair arms and licked his lips. He had that peculiar vibrating feeling in his chest, and his mind was spilling over with plots, criminals, alibis and storylines, both fact and fiction – so much so, he couldn't think straight.

'Are you coming, Frank?'

'Yes. Right. I'm coming, lass.'

He didn't say much. He ate the meal; he didn't know what it was. He returned briefly to the armchair. At nine o'clock, he said he was going to bed. At twenty minutes past, he was asleep. He went into a deep sleep. He didn't hear Irene come to bed at half-past ten, read her book for about half an hour and then switch off the light. She heard him breathing very deeply and very slowly ... and touched his hand and his cheek gently to reassure herself that he was all right.

SEVENTEEN

At 4.57 exactly, that Monday morning, 5th January, Spence's eyes clicked open. He was immediately awake, and surprised he should be so alert so quickly. The room was as black as a witch's cat. He switched the bedside light on briefly and turned his head to see the clock. He turned it off. He could hear Irene breathing next to him. Then it all came to him. It burst into his consciousness, blocking out everything else – the explanation of the trout, and more, *loads* more … the whole case about Kass. It was obvious. He pushed himself up to a sitting position and sat there, momentarily dazed. He peeled back the blankets and got out of bed. He desperately wanted to waken Irene and share it with her, but on reflection, he reckoned the way things were at the moment she would have been less than pleased.

In the dark, he collected up his clothes and the contents of his pockets, went out of the bedroom and quietly closed the door. He tried to think clearly about organizing himself, to save time, but his mind was far too busy. He washed, shaved and dressed in very few minutes. He would have enjoyed a cup of tea but he didn't think of it. He was eager to get to the police station. There were details to check up on. He unlocked the back door, switched off the lights and went out.

It was still dark and the roads were deserted. He arrived at the station at twenty to six. The PC on reception looked at the clock, gave him a funny look, but waved him through. Spence had some urgent reading to do. He went straight down to the office he had been using, pulled out the SOCO report from the drawer and got stuck into it. He had read it all before but needed to check that everything fitted. He pulled out a sheet of A4 and made notes as he went along.

At eight o'clock he went out to the vending machine for a drink. He came back with it and began hunting through the pile of papers on the desk, hoping to find the file from SOCO about the incidents in the café and the ice-cream factory. They weren't there. He flopped down in the chair and leaned backwards. He rubbed his chin and yawned. It was the first time he'd yawned in months. He looked at his watch: it was 8.20. He reached forward and made two phone calls: one to Leeds and one to Irene to explain where he was. He had to waken her so he hadn't been missed, which slightly disappointed him. Then he went down to the briefing room. There was a solitary WPC in there. He left a message with her for Gold, then came back to the office to wait.

Only a minute or two later, there was a knock at the door.

'Come in,' he said enthusiastically.

It was Gold. She came in, all smiles.

'I didn't know you were due back, sir,' she said brightly. 'Have a good Christmas?'

'Yes. Have you checked off that number 122 against Edmund Symington?'

'Yes, sir. And I can't find any connection. Nothing he's got has a 122 in it. Telephone number, army number, bank account, mobile. I've looked at everything I can think of.'

He sighed.

'Hmm. Right.'

'Didn't know you were coming in, sir.'

'Not sure I'm supposed to here. You remember that foot-print in the doorway at the café?'

'Yes, sir.'

'Have you had a report from SOCO about it? Didn't they specify the shoe size?'

'We've had a report about that break-in, sir, yes. I don't remember anything about the shoe size.'

'If the footprint is from a size eight shoe, then I know where the Persian Salamander is hidden.'

Gold stared straight at him. Her mouth dropped open. '*What*?' She licked her lips and then said, 'How do you know *that*, sir?'

His mouth tightened.

'It's ... what I do,' he said impatiently. 'Now buzz off and find the report ... it'll be in there ... and let me know. I'll be in the super's office.'

Gold rushed off.

Spence made his way purposefully down the corridor to the superintendent's office. He knocked at the door.

'Come in.'

Spence pushed open the door.

The superintendent raised his head and his spectacle lenses flashed in the light like Himmler. He was standing over his desk shuffling through some letters.

'What is it? Oh, it's you. What are you doing here?'

'I think I know where the missing Persian Salamander is.'

'Oh?' the superintendent said, staring at him briefly then resuming the search. He picked up a bundle of envelopes, shuffled through them, glancing pointlessly at the address on each one in turn as he thought out what he wanted to say. 'That's that Iraqi jewel thing, isn't it?' he muttered casually. 'Well, that *wasn't* in your brief. What are you doing wasting your time with that? You were briefed to find a murderer.

Anyway, it's in America, isn't it? You can't go flying off to the States … can't fork out for that, lad.'

'No need, sir. If the footprint at the café is from a size eight shoe, I know exactly where it is.'

He wrinkled his nose.

'Hmmm. Well be that as it may,' he said. He sat down behind the desk and pointed to a chair.

Spence sat down on the chair opposite.

'Look here, Spence,' he continued, 'I was going to write you. I have a long, tedious letter about the case against Symington from the CPS.'

'Yes. Well, I'll deal with it, sir, if you want me to.'

'I don't want you dragging it out and putting endless claims in for time … wasted … arguing the toss with them.'

'If we recover the Persian Salamander—'

'That's not in your brief. I never told you to go running after that.'

'If *I* recover the Persian Salamander then, in my *own* time, I suppose I am eligible for the reward. A hundred thousand euros, I think it is.'

The superintendent suddenly looked up. He blinked and rubbed his chin.

'Ah well, it *is* a crime. As you were on police time, you couldn't accept a reward while being paid for public service. You wouldn't *want* to, would you?'

Spence concealed a smile.

There was a knock at the door.

'Come in.'

It was Gold.

'Excuse me, sir. May I pass on some urgent information to Mr Spence?'

The superintendent wrinkled up his nose then grudgingly nodded.

She looked at Spence with a big smile. 'It is a gent's size eight, sir.'

'Ah!' he said. 'Thank you.'

They exchanged grins.

The door closed.

'What's that all about?'

'That wraps up the case against him.'

'Against who? What are you talking about?'

'Edmund Symington is a captain in the Catering Corps in the regular army. Ronnie Kass was in his unit ... a humble private. I believe that they, and maybe with others, stole the Persian Salamander from the Glass Palace in Baghdad. Anyway, it was smuggled out of Iraq in a sack of sugar and left safely stored under guard at his unit's HQ in the UK, while he came home to Castlecombe on seven days' leave, and Kass on his discharge also came here ... no doubt to look after his interests. They were presumably intent on making arrangements to sell the jewel as soon as possible, and to that end they met up with Basil Van de Meyer.'

'Is he still around?'

'They met for a meal up at the Castlecombe House Hotel. Don't know what transpired ... probably nothing firm. Two days later, unexpectedly, Symington had stomach pains – he had appendicitis. He was rushed to hospital and he had to have his appendix out. He or his wife would have informed his CO, in the course of which he learned that his unit was being contracted and that the powers that be had disposed of the foodstuffs and cooking equipment that had been brought back from Iraq in a "short notice" auction somewhere. When he heard this, Symington panicked. He discharged himself from hospital to begin the search for the sack of sugar in which he had hidden the Salamander. I have a CCTV photograph of him taken in Manchester, in the yard of the wholesalers who bought the sugar. He is doubled up with pain – I thought it was an animal at first. This was four days after the op ... the night Kass was murdered.'

'So he couldn't have murdered Kass, then?'

'He was in Manchester. He doesn't know we have this photograph of him. But he couldn't admit to it anyway. He didn't want to admit he was breaking into a warehouse in the search for the fabulous Salamander he had stolen, if he could avoid it.'

'Did he find it then?'

'Oh yes. He eventually found the sack of sugar with it in – I don't know *where* – from one of the traders that had bought the sugar from the wholesaler ... he would have stolen the list – but I know *when*. It was on 22 December. He was sailing home in his car, in the early hours, with it safely in his boot, still inside the paper sack ... the one he had sewn it into, while in Iraq. If there hadn't been a few grains of sugar dropped in the boot, I might never have known. Where he finally deposited it, it may have stayed hidden for many years, if he had been found guilty of murder! Anyway, I was with Gold, waiting for him to return, outside his house that morning. He pulled up to the front of his house but when he saw her uniform, he raced off. If he'd been stopped, he certainly would know that his car would have been searched and the jewel found. So as he was approaching Rabbitspaw Bridge, he had an idea. He stopped at the top of the bridge, dropped the sack with the Salamander over the wall into the water, knowing that the water wouldn't harm the jewel, and that it would be safely hidden until he was in a position to retrieve it. He then dashed off and a mile or so later slowed down sufficiently to allow us to catch him.'

'How do you know he dumped it over the bridge? Did you see him? Did he admit it? Has it since been found?'

'No, sir. He didn't tell us, of course. He didn't admit anything. I arrested him and he has been in custody ever since.'

'Well, how can you possibly know all that?'

'Bear with me, sir. I didn't know it at the time, but on Saturday, 27 December – that's five days after Symington dropped the jewel in the sack of sugar into the stream, I went to Castlecombe House Hotel and had a most delightful meal. A poacher had providentially set nets forty yards upstream of the bridge, and then at the bridge itself, thus preventing a particular fish from escaping the very sweet water that had been created by the sugar dissolving through the paper sack. For five days, that fish had an intensive diet of sweet water to swim about in. The properties of the water affect the flavour of fish, of course, and I was one of the fortunate diners to experience the unique taste of that particular trout.'

The superintendent looked bombed. His eyes glazed, his mouth dropped opened, he put his hand to his chin.

'But how do you ... how can you know that?'

'Because five days after that, on New Year's Day, I tasted a similar trout caught forty yards *upstream* from there, where the water had *not* been affected by the sugar and was *not*, therefore, so uniquely sweet.'

The superintendent rubbed his scratchy little chin hard, then shook his head.

'You never cease to amaze me, lad! You never cease to amaze me!'

Spence sighed.

Superintendent Marriott stood up. He walked over to the window, looked out of it momentarily and then turned back.

'Hmmm. Well ... you'd better get it out of the water smartish, before your poacher beats you to it.'

'It will have sunk to the bottom of the pond, out of sight. Should be safe enough. But, anyway, I have already phoned the Underwater Search and Rescue Squad at Leeds and asked them to send out a couple of divers and an inflatable. They should be here any time now.'

'Very well. Carry on. You'd better be right about all this, Spence. There's all this embarrassment with the CPS and the magistrates,' he growled. 'You'll have to sort it out with them. All right, you may have got him for the robbery – I never really thought Symington was a cold-blooded murderer. But we are no further forward finding the one who did. Hmmm. And I thought I'd got rid of you. Hmmm. What are your lines of enquiry then?'

'The clue Kass left for us.'

'You mean that number chalked in the dust?' he sniffed. '*That all?* You'll be lucky to turn that up if you haven't found it by now. This is costing a fortune. I'll give you twenty-four hours.'

Gold and Spence went into the forensic theatre, normally only used for post mortems. Ron Todd nodded at them and closed the door.

Facing them was Dr Chester, holding a Stanley knife over a large wet paper sack, which was assuming the place of a body on the elevated stainless-steel table.

She looked up.

'Just in time. You'll be pleased to know there were prints on the sack – we managed to retrieve them despite the soaking. Symington's, of course, among others.'

Spence nodded and smiled. He was impatient to see inside the sack, to make sure that the Persian Salamander was indeed there, that his abilities of deduction had not been diminished by the shock of being shot at, the subsequent operation and his physical and mental recovery, followed by two years away from real crime. He knew he was going to look remarkably ridiculous if the sack only contained sugar!

Dr Chester moved quickly. She put the blade of the knife at the top of the sack and deliberately scored a single clean cut down to the bottom. A small amount of water dribbled out. The sack opened an inch or so exposing a strip of white sugar that reflected brightly in the powerful overhead light.

Dr Chester thrust her white rubber-gloved hand through the long slit into the paper sack and rummaged around, just as she might in the cavity of a corpse.

A click and a glaring flash of white light the intensity of lightning momentarily illuminated the room, causing Gold to gasp. Her hands jerked and she looked behind her.

Todd smiled apologetically and pointed at the camera he was holding by her ear.

Spence edged forward. He licked his lips nervously and watched the doctor's white coat-sleeve stop waggling, stiffen and then slowly withdraw something of irregular shape, loosely bound in white plastic wrapping. She held it up. A shower of wet sugar dropped on the bag.

The camera flashed again.

Spence licked his bottom lip while holding his breath.

She turned and lowered the object on to a dissecting table covered with a white plastic-coated top, marked out in a black chequered grid. She peered closely down at the discovery.

'Hmmm. It's approximately forty-two centimetres long. the width varies between twelve down to three or two at the tail,' she said.

Ron Todd noted it on a pad with a felt-tip pen.

She then began slowly to unwrap it. There were several layers of the plastic covering.

Ron Todd returned to the camera and snapped away at every revelation.

A bright blue colour began to show through the wrapping.

Spence breathed out, nodded and smiled.

He heard Gold gasp as a small, delicately carved golden foot of the small creature was uncovered.

The doctor pulled away the final cover.

Everybody's eyes homed in on the blinding show of diamonds and rubies set in lapis lazuli sculpted in the form of a reptile. The diamonds and rubies twinkled in the powerful overhead light.

There were gasps and then silence.

Todd busily continued clicking away and the diamonds reflected the flashes as if they were in themselves alive.

Eventually, Spence straightened up, sighed and smiled.

'Thank you, Doctor. I'll make arrangements to have this … jewel collected by a security firm in the next hour.'

EIGHTEEN

Spence pushed in a new tape and switched on the recorder. 'January 5th, 12.15. Interview of Edmund Symington by Frank Spence. Present Miss Keys and WPC Gold,' he said and then he turned to the man seated opposite him. 'I asked Miss Keys to attend, Mr Symington, because we have now uncovered evidence that you, with others, stole the jewel known as the Persian Salamander, that you smuggled it out of Iraq in a sack of sugar and that you tried to sell it to Basil Van de Meyer.'

Symington's mouth tightened but he said nothing.

Spence reckoned it must have been quite a shock to Symington and he reckoned the man had controlled his reactions remarkably well.

'In addition,' he continued, 'there are six charges of breaking and entering into food-preparing premises that we are aware of ... In search of it, I assume ... Other charges from other forces are being prepared and will be added as the information reaches us.'

Symington recovered well and stared at him impassively.

'Have you anything to say?' Spence added.

Symington looked at Miss Keys, who returned the look without any expression. Then he shook his head.

'No.'

'Are you pleading guilty?'

'Certainly not. You can't link me to *that*,' Symington said forcibly. 'Anyway, there's no such thing as the Persian Salamander. There *was* a story going around Baghdad about a famous jewel of that name but it was stolen and broken up years ago, in the fifties. It is something the Iraqis made up so that they could accuse the West of looting ... It's a fairy story.'

'We'll see.'

'You'd have to produce the thing to make a case that I'd stolen it. Huh! You could *never* do that.'

Spence turned to Gold and held out his hand. She opened the file in front of her, shuffled through several photographs and handed him one. He silently pushed it across the table to Symington. His eyelids lifted almost imperceptibly when he looked at it.

'It was taken out of Dingle pond under Rabbitspaw Bridge about two hours ago,' Spence added. 'And it's going back to Iraq, where it belongs, as soon as I can organize it.'

Symington shook his head and pushed the photograph back. He was visibly shaken.

'There is more evidence. Sugar in the boot of your car ... The sack in which it was found had been in your car until you dropped it over the bridge into Dingle pond just before I arrested you. Your fingerprints on the sack ...'

Symington shrugged.

'Don't know how it got there. My wife and I are always having picnics in the summer ... must have spilled some.'

'A shoe print in a café you broke into. That was careless. Matches your shoe exactly.'

'There must be a lot of people out there wearing shoes like mine.'

'And sugar in the welt of the shoes you were wearing

when you were arrested, and specks vacuumed off your suit. You must be a very worried man. A charge of murder hanging over you and now a charge of robbery ... major robbery. You might never see daylight again.'

'You've got to make them stick, Inspector.'

'Oh we'll make them stick all right,' Spence said forcefully. 'But I could make life a *bit* easier for you. I could show you a way of getting *off* the murder charge, by pleading guilty to the robbery ...'

Miss Keys whipped off her glasses. 'Inspector Spence, you really can't put a proposition like that. It's most improper. It implies that he's guilty. Mr Symington is an innocent man—'

Spence put up his hand.

'An innocent man who's going down for murder if he's not careful,' he said robustly. 'Miss Keys, I am not a police inspector. I am not a member of the police. I am simply Frank Norman Spence, ordinary citizen of this town, *employed* by the police, but not *of* the police. WPC Gold here represents the police. I could ask her to leave, if you wish. But it isn't really necessary. Hear me out. I was a policeman serving here for twenty-seven years. I know the ropes. There is enough evidence to find your client guilty of robbery and the other associated offences, and there *is* a photograph, not a good photograph, a photograph taken at exactly the time Ronnie Kass was in that miserable little flat gasping his last breath. It's a still from a CCTV camera in Manchester with a date and time on it. Mr Symington, if you are prepared to plead guilty to the charge of robbery of the Persian Salamander, I am prepared to accept that that photograph is of you, and withdraw the charge against you for the murder of Ronnie Kass.'

'That smacks of a very contrived deal, Mr Spence,' Miss Keys said indignantly.

'Not a deal. A proposition to save time and pain. You don't have to accept it. You could stand trial for murder and take your chance.'

She looked at Symington, who remained expressionless, turned away and ran his hand through his hair. He didn't seem to know where to look.

'I'd need to see the photograph,' Miss Keys said.

Spence nodded at Gold, who produced the blurred and grainy still sent by email by Manchester police endorsed with the date and time: '15.12.03. 1832.'

Miss Keys showed it to Symington. They looked at it without comment.

After a moment, she looked up.

'Can I have some time to consult my client?'

Spence smiled.

'Wish I could have done that, sir,' Gold said, her eyes shining.

'What?'

'You, sir, working all that out from a few grains of sugar in the car and a footprint, that CCTV picture and the trout and everything.'

'You *will* do, one day. It'll come to you. If you set your heart to it. It's merely a matter of experience. I'm not even conscious I'm doing it. Habit, I think. Repetition … I've done it so many times before. My mind … sort of … takes *me* over. Analyses all the reasons and facts as to why things *are* the way they *are*, and then systematically tries every sequence of them until there is only one logical one remaining and that's got to be it, however crackpot or unlikely it may seem to be.'

'Hmmm. Well, why hasn't it worked finding Kass's murderer, sir?'

'Because I haven't quite enough information,' he said patiently.

'Well, how will you … How will your mind know when you *have*?'

He smiled. He didn't know the answer. He didn't attempt a reply.

'The super has given me twenty-four hours,' he said. 'So I've got to get a move on. I'll have to cover the ground again … have another look at everything. There'll be some little thing we've overlooked. There'll be an answer there some-where. There always is. Firstly, I need to look again at the alibis of the people involved with him.'

'The time of Kass's death was determined by old Mrs Turvey hearing him turn off his CD player, wasn't it, sir?'

'The music stopped playing abruptly at 6.30 on Monday, 15 December. This was further supported by the Lees recalling that they had served him a takeaway soon after they opened the shop at six. I wonder …'

'At 6.30, I was here serving in the shop,' Mrs Lee asserted.

Her husband stood just behind her, his gnarled hands holding her at the waist.

'And I was cooking,' he said. 'She couldn't serve anything if it wasn't cooked.'

Spence nodded.

'And you are sure it was Monday 15 December?'

'That was the last time he came in,' she said, her face like stone.

'At six o'clock. On the dot. Just as we opened. He was always waiting. The first customer,' Lee added. 'Chicken chow-mein.'

'You served him, five or ten minutes later, he paid and he walked straight out of the shop?'

'Yes,' Mrs Lee said.

'You didn't happen to see which direction he took?'

'Yes,' she said. 'He crossed the road. I suppose he went straight to his flat.'

'And both of you were here and you stayed open here serving until ... what time?'

'Ten o'clock. We close at ten.'

'You can prove it?'

Lee shrugged. 'There were customers coming in and out all the time—'

'It was busy ... very busy,' she added. 'We are the only takeaway open on a Monday night.'

Spence nodded.

'Thank you.'

'Six thirty?' Mrs Carrington said thoughtfully. 'Well, Mr Spence. We'd be having our tea and watching the news on the television. They say it's bad for the indigestion, don't they? But ... it was a Monday, wasn't it ... yes. That's where we would be, in the kitchen, in the back, having tea.'

'Can anybody vouch for it, Mrs Carrington?'

'Yes, of course. We can vouch for each other. Russell and I could never be separated from each other for long. I know you haven't always seen us at our best, Mr Spence, but, well, you have to make allowances. Russell has had a very disadvantaged bringing up. He was backwards at school. Failed his eleven plus. His mother used to beat him, even when he was late into his teens. He was naughty ... only naughtiness, you know. Nothing serious or criminal or anything like that. She struggled to bring him up on her own. Goodness knows what happened to his father. He never speaks of him. When she was alive, she never spoke about him either. Apparently he was something of a tearaway. I believe his father was a drunk, you know. When I met Russell, he wouldn't talk to anyone. It took me and a lot of patience to bring him out of his shell.'

'But no-one actually was with you at 6.30, the night of the murder, 15 December?'

'No,' Mrs Carrington said, fluttering her eyelashes. 'And you are not to believe all those ridiculous stories about me being upstairs with Ronnie Kass during the afternoons …'

The door opened. Mrs Symington put her head through the gap. When she saw it was Spence, her eyebrows shot up and her face tightened.

'Well, well, well,' she said tartly. 'You managed to find *something* to pin on my husband then. I don't know how you've the cheek to call here. Your men left early this morning. They left the kitchen in a tip. However, I am pleased to say they didn't find a single incriminating thing!'

Spence breathed out through pursed lips.

'I'm glad to hear it, Mrs Symington. But I am here on another matter.'

'What, *more* questions?'

'Just one.'

'If it's about the fire in the incinerator, that was an old suit of Edmund's he wanted burning … *not* because it was covered with Ronnie Kass's blood!'

'No,' he replied promptly. 'It was because it was all stuck up with *sugar*!'

She glared angrily at him. His reply had clearly surprised her. 'No. Not at all. It was the suit he had been tinkering with the car in … It had … oil stains on it.'

'Well, why burn it? Why not just throw it in the dustbin?'

Her face went scarlet.

While she was thinking of an answer, Spence said: 'No, I

came to ask you what you were doing in the early evening of Monday, 15 December.'

'My husband was in hospital. I would be visiting him, of course.'

Spence shook his head. 'No, Mrs Symington. He had discharged himself the day before ... the Sunday. I know, for a fact, because at the time he was in Manchester breaking into a warehouse.'

Her mouth dropped open.

'The question is, where were *you*?'

'Here, I suppose.'

'On your own.'

'Of course.'

Spence returned to the station.

That was it. The alibis were about as useless as they could be, and nothing new had been uncovered. Nine of the precious twenty-four hours had been wasted. He would be loath to leave the murder unsolved for someone else one day, hopefully, to have the pleasure of solving. But maybe he'd done enough at it. Maybe he had simply got too close to it. The old story about couldn't see the wood for trees. He wondered if there was anything in the forensic report that he had overlooked. He resolved to take it home that night and read through it again. He had already been through it twice but he didn't want to be beaten.

He arrived home at six o'clock. Irene greeted him with a smile and a kiss. He was very pleased, but wondered what was wrong. He had tea, watched the television, but didn't see anything. He looked at the screen but his mind was still on the case. He was wondering why he let Symington off the charge of murder so easily. Oh, it was all right. He wasn't guilty, but he wondered why he was getting so soft. Ten years ago, he wouldn't have done that. He retired early and read the report in bed. Slept like a top. Next morning, as he munched through his All Bran, he decided to get back to his own writing. Blow the super. He had read the forensic report on Kass's body, clothes and flat. The deadline was half-past nine that morning. There was no way he could see he was going to come up with some new evidence in two hours.

He had a shower, a shave and dressed, then went upstairs to the little box room and switched on his computer. As it was loading up, Irene came in with a beaker of tea and a letter.

'The post,' she said. 'One from Czechoslovakia, I think,' she said, with her eyebrows raised.

'Thanks, love,' he said, and looked at the big foreign stamp on the corner of the envelope.

She turned to go.

He fished round for his penknife, found it and began to slit open the envelope.

'Who do we know in Czechoslovakia?'

She turned back.

He opened it.

'Ah. It's from that publisher in Prague. It's a cheque acknowledging rights to publish in Czech. Hmmm. It's a lot of noughts in Koruna.'

'Great. How much is that?'

He shook his head.

'I'll ring the bank. It'll be a few quid.'

'Great. I need some shoes,' she said and wandered out of the room, carrying a beaker of coffee.

He didn't reply. He watched her leave and shook his head. At 9.05 he phoned the bank.

A young voice answered.

'Northern Bank. Can I help you?'

'Yes. I've received a cheque from a firm in Czechoslovakia. I was wondering … well, how much it was worth, and—'

'You need our foreign desk. You need to speak to our Mr Turvey.'

'Thank you,' Spence said. He nodded. That was good. He knew Turvey well enough by now. It would be easy to speak to him about it.

'I am putting you through.'

There was a click and the familiar friendly voice said: 'Extension 122. Raymond Turvey, foreign desk manager here. Can I help you?'

122. The number rattled round Spence's head. The hair on the back of his neck stood up. He couldn't speak.

'Hello. Can I help you?' he could hear Turvey saying.

Spence put his hand on the telephone cradle and cancelled the call. He then dialled the police station.

An hour later, he arrived at the Northern Bank accompanied by Gold. They went to the enquiry desk and asked to see Mr Turvey and were immediately shown into a small office next to the entry to the lift.

Mr Turvey stood up when they entered, all smiles.

'Nice to see you, Mr Spence and you … miss. Please sit down. How can I help you?'

Spence began soberly.

'I have reason to believe that you can help us with our enquiries regarding the murder of Ronnie Kass.'

Turvey blinked, but continued to smile. 'In what way?'

'Firstly, you can tell us where you were at the time of his murder.'

'Oh? I was at home … My wife would be able to confirm that.'

'And when *was* that exactly, Mr Turvey?'

'Monday night, 15 December … around 6.30.'

'How did you know that?'

'You mentioned it when you visited my mother.'

'No, sir. I interviewed your mother the day the body was found – that was Wednesday, 17th. I didn't know myself when he was murdered until the post-mortem report came in on Friday 19th. But you are spot on with the day and the time.'

'Well, I must have read it in the newspaper then.'

'You couldn't have. It was deliberately withheld from the media.'

He looked stunned.

'Only one person knew the exact time and date of the murder ... and that was the murderer,' Spence said ominously.

Turvey's face changed.

Spence slowly shook his head. 'Your mother pushed you just that little bit too far, didn't she?' he said quietly.

Turvey slumped down into the chair and lowered his head on to his chest.

Spence could see that his eyes were moist.

After a moment, Turvey said, 'I couldn't do any more for her. She was ringing me up six and seven times a day or when I got home at night. There was always something she wanted ... or there was something wrong ... or she had dropped something on the floor and couldn't reach it ... or a light bulb needed changing ... or a noise that was driving her mad ... My life wasn't my own any more. We could never go on holiday or even away for a day. My wife was going to leave me.'

'We have already closely interviewed your wife. She knew nothing of the murder. There's a policewoman with her now. Now that she knows, I understand she says she'll stand by you.'

'Oh?' he said and looked up, surprised.

'Your house is being searched by police officers as we speak, and we'll need to look round your office here and your desk.'

Turvey's face suddenly hardened like rock. His lips tightened. 'You'll have to prove it, Spence. Every bit of the way.'

'Oh, we've got proof already, Mr Spence. We've found the suit, shirt and shoes you were wearing when you murdered Ronnie Kass, and the kitchen knife you stuck into him that you left in a suitcase at your mother's ... on top of the wardrobe.'

Turvey lowered his head into his chest again.

Spence stood up, looked at Gold and nodded urgently towards Turvey.

She stood up, cleared her throat and began: 'Raymond Turvey, I am arresting you on suspicion of murder. You do not have to say anything ...'

Spence made a point of arriving at the office early the following morning. He wanted to check that all the statements, witness recordings, photographs and so on were all in order for the CPS. He wanted to brief Gold so that he could leave everything with her, return home and continue writing his book.

The phone rang. It was the switchboard with a call from Zack.

'Hello there, Mr Spence,' he said loudly. He sounded to be in very good form. 'I see'd the papers. The whisper round the track is that you've got a chap for that murder. S'marvellous. You haven't lost the magic touch, I see.'

'That was quick, Zack. Who told you?'

'Aye, and you've found that big jewel Salamander thing too and got the chap, Symington. Thing is, Mr Spence. I thought you'd like to know that the Weasel's back. As soon as the news broke late last night, he was back with the big girl, Gloria, from the butcher's, before you could say "They're off". He just phoned me to put a bet on tomorrow's big race, and he said that it's all great between them again. It's like a second honeymoon. He had something going in Whitby, but the husband came back unexpectedly from Reykjavik so it turned out well for him. I thought you'd like to know that Gloria spotted the picture of a man on the front page of the *Northern Daily*. She said it was that Captain Symington. He *was* the chap who put the frighteners on her and was prepared to offer Weasel £1,000 to wear de blinkers and stop him talking about what he saw and heard in Castlecombe House. Course, he wouldn't say it in court, but I thought it might help you to know that it was definitely him.'

'Thank you, Zack.'

Later that morning, Spence drove Gold up on to the moors and turned at the crossroads on the back road towards Whitby. He went down Hare Lane to Rabbitspaw Bridge and turned left into the layby next to it. He pulled on the brake and switched off the ignition.

'You'll be acting as continuity officer in this case,' he said to her. 'So I'm showing you the exact spot where Edmund Symington dropped off the sack of sugar with the Persian Salamander in it … so you know what you're talking about, if you're asked about it.'

Gold nodded and pulled on her gloves.

They got out of the car and walked back the few paces up to the icy road and then to the brow of the little humpback bridge. It was cold and quite breezy. The evergreen trees rustled and the wind whistled around the little bridge. There was not a soul to be seen.

'Now he'd stop his car here on this very spot, open the tailgate, hump the sack on to the wall and push it over.'

'Yes, sir.'

He looked over the wall of the bridge at the stream of water below. 'Mmm. About sixteen foot drop, I suppose.'

She came up to the low wall and looked over it.

'And how deep is the water, sir?'

'About four feet, I guess.'

'Mmmm,' she said and leaned over the wall a bit further. Then, suddenly, she screwed up her face and said, 'What's that smell, sir?'

Spence frowned, leaned over the wall and looked down at the flowing water and the foliage on the bank waving in the breeze. He sniffed and true enough, much to his surprise, there was an unusual smell. It smelled like something cooking. He couldn't imagine from where it might have originated. There was nobody for miles.

She stared at him knowingly.

'Oh, I know what it is, sir. *It's curry.*'

Spence stared at her briefly, confused.

'Yes,' she said confidently. 'Sure enough. It's curried haddock.'

His mouth dropped open. He sniffed. He had to agree.

Her eyes glowed. 'I told you before, sir. Your friend wouldn't desert you. Been with you all the time. It's the spirit of Wally Walpole here to lend a hand.'